FALSE PRETENCES

Lee Langley was born in India and spent her childhood there. Her last three novels were set in India. *Changes of Address* and *A House in Pondicherry* were shortlisted for the Hawthornden Prize, and *Persistent Rumours* won both the Commonwealth Writers' Prize for Best Novel (Eurasia) and the Writers' Guild of Great Britain Best Novel Award. She is a Fellow of the Royal Society of Literature.

ALSO BY LEE LANGLEY

Lee Langley

FALSE PRETENCES

V

VINTAGE

Published by Vintage 1999

2 4 6 8 10 9 7 5 3 1

First published in Great Britain by
Chatto & Windus in 1998

Vintage
Random House, 20 Vauxhall Bridge Road,
London SW1V 2SA

Random House Australia (Pty) Limited
20 Alfred Street, Milsons Point, Sydney
New South Wales 2061, Australia

Random House New Zealand Limited
18 Poland Road, Glenfield, Auckland 10,
New Zealand

Random House South Africa (Pty) Limited
Endulini, 5A Jubilee Road, Parktown 2193,
South Africa

The Random House Group Limited Reg. No. 954009
www.randomhouse.co.uk

A CIP catalogue record for this book
is available from the British Library

ISBN 0 09 927315 2

Papers used by Random House are natural, recyclable
products made from wood grown in sustainable forests.
The manufacturing processes conform to the environ-
mental regulations of the country of origin

Printed and bound by CPI Antony Rowe, Eastbourne

For Gerry and Val

Contents

Brocken's Spectre

———————

Brocken's Spectre

They sprawled about the overgrown garden, flopping
untidily, like bundles of cast-off clothing – two men,
three women, children, a baby – and the heat lay over
them, settling into folds in the Welsh hillside, gathering
stickily at the backs of knees, inner elbows, necks,
blanketing the earth, so that movement meant effort,
fighting gravity. A tide of warm air lapped the recum-
bent bodies. They lay, sipping white wine, drowsing,
whiling away the time till dinner.

It was early in the year for such heat, the leaves still
bright, the flowers taken by surprise, the grass juicy.
With time there would be a withering, a drying, a smell
of scorched things, but now, at the very beginning of
summer, the heat came like a spell and breathed over
them.

Threads link these people. Two are husband and wife,
well pleased by the miracle they have conjured between
them; they study their creation, awed by the smallness of
toes, the transparency of ears, tracing curves of cheek
and brow. Conscious of the fragility of an infant skull
whose bones are not yet knitted, the mother holds a

protective palm against the pulsing membrane of the fontanelle, visualises the small, soft bones squeezed in the birth canal, expanding in the light and air, hears again the gasping breath that proclaimed, 'I'm here!' She strokes the unformed nose, touches a fingernail no bigger than a lentil.

In a sagging, mildewed deckchair is a small, dark woman whose children are busy nearby, tracking ants through the grass. In cooler weather she could find it in her to resent her hostess: the Flower Power frocks, brown rice and CND badges, along with a Harley Street obstetrician for the birth. High-mindedness has apparently ruled out the purchase of a decent garden chair or two. Marie-Hélène shifts fretfully and gives a passing thought to her own looming domestic upheaval; possible rupture, a trip home to France . . .

Nearby, a younger woman is curled up on a rug under a tree, eyes closed. She too has turbulent thoughts, not unconnected with the man who lies a little way off, pretending to read yesterday's newspaper yellowed and brittled by the sun, in reality slipping in and out of a wine-tinged doze. Newly met, these two are still engaged in the early steps of what might or might not lead to something more. He is drawn by her silences, her containment; she is tempted by his vigour, opening herself to the possibility of passion. His skin, already brown from the sun, has a silky down of fine golden hairs. At the table, earlier, his arm brushed hers and she felt a small shock, as though each tiny hair carried an electric charge which detonated inside her. She breathes slowly, her face calm as always.

Meanwhile, the ants are busy carrying off sugar from abandoned tea mugs, prising the dried grains free of the porcelain, running a supply chain through the clover to the courtyard flagstones, unaware of hovering children with bright, curious eyes. The hillside slumbers.

Far off, at the bottom of the hill, something is moving, a tiny figure on a bicycle, a speck on the landscape, coming towards them. The wheeled centaur moves slowly along the lane, then stops. Sunlight flashes on glass, dazzling them.

'Whoever it is, he's having a look at us,' Patrick says.

The figure turns off the lane and comes, very slowly, up the track to the cottage. They watch from their green plateau, sitting up to observe more closely, as the blurred shape resolves itself into man and bike. When the track grows steeper, he gets off and, bent low, wheels the machine, seeming to urge it forward. Boy rather than man, he is tall, skinny, very fair, his pale hair flopping onto small acid glasses that reflect the sky when he raises his head and comes to a stop, breathing deeply.

'Hallo!' Patrick calls out. 'I'm afraid this track doesn't

lead anywhere, you'll have to go back the way you came.'

The boy unclips a metal bottle from the bike. 'I need some water. If I could just get a refill . . .'

Jan climbs to her feet. 'Of course!' She takes the bottle and goes into the house, the Indian cotton caftan swirling around her bare feet.

He stands waiting, wiping his face on his sleeve. When he takes off the sunglasses they see that his eyes are as pale as pebbles in stream water, lighter than the sky. His jeans are bleached, rubbed threadbare at the knees. Something about his paleness gathers the sunlight to him so that he seems to stand out from the surrounding greenery as if spotlit. He glances round the group, not quite smiling, but giving an impression of amiability. Patrick, aware that the rest of them hold wine glasses, waves his own enquiringly.

'How about a glass of this stuff to help you on your way?'

The boy props the bike against a tree. 'Great,' he says, 'thanks.' He squats, savouring the wine, pressing the cool glass against his temple, glancing around. 'Nice place.'

Patrick waves a dismissive hand. 'The roof will cave in one of these days.' He gives one of his ironical, smiling shrugs.

Jan wanders back from the kitchen, screwing on the bottle top, and sees them talking, the new arrival stretched out on the grass, head propped on hand. Patrick turns towards her as she reaches them. 'This is Jan,' he says, 'that's the baby, by the gooseberry bush, appropriately.' He goes round the group, introducing everyone: Marie-Hélène; her two children; Stuart, an old friend; and Susan Ross, a new one, a colleague and fellow-teacher.

'Nick,' the boy says, nodding.

'Short for Nicholas?' Marie-Hélène pronounces it the French way.

'For Niccolò. I had ambitious parents.'

Susan notes the past tense; orphans have a way of recognising one another from casual clues. Jan hands back the water bottle, ready to wave the traveller on his way, but Patrick has already refilled the boy's glass, offering advice on the route to the next town.

For the ants crossing the flagstones, catastrophe comes without warning; the children, bored with watching, squash them beneath their fingers, flattening the sugar caravan in mid-journey. Survivors scatter, directionless, their occupation gone.

Time passes. Glasses are replenished, small confidences extended. Marie-Hélène's husband has been held up in London, directing a documentary that – as is often the case – requires weekend shooting. 'He'll be here quite soon.'

Stuart writes obituaries for a national newspaper: 'Not quite the career I planned . . .'

These and other facts emerge with an ease that surprises Jan, but the boy no longer seems a stranger. Graceful, responsive, he admires the baby, and permits the children to daub his face with finger-paints. They rim his eyes with crimson like an Indian god, decorate his hollow cheeks with dark stripes. The sun has left the lower reaches of the hillside and the shadows creep up towards the house.

Marie-Hélène's children leap like rabbits, waving at their shadows, thrown long and attenuated against the steep grassy slope by the setting sun.

'If you're lucky, you might see Brocken's Spectre,' Patrick tells them.

'Who was Brocken?' Susan calls over.

'What, not who. It's a high point in the Harz mountains in Germany – where the witches are supposed to hold their revels on Walpurgis Night. The spectre's just an optical illusion when your shadow falls on a moist surface – thick mist, or dewy grass – while the sun's setting. You see rings of luminous colours round the edge of your shadow.' The children are stilled: they stand, staring at their shadows thrown against the green slope, complaining when no spectre appears to them. 'Not damp enough. Or the angle's wrong. No Brocken, no spectre. Tough luck, kids.'

'At least it'll be easier going, in the cool.' The boy flexes his shoulders, breathing deeply. 'Lovely air.' He pauses, sniffing appreciatively. 'Something smells good.'

The aroma of Welsh lamb, anointed with herbs and garlic, roasting slowly in the Aga, drifts from the kitchen. Jan is aware of an awkward fact: the village, when he reaches it, will have packed up for the night. What will he do for food while they sit here gorging? She ignores the small nudge of guilt: not her problem. The boy crouches by the infant's basket: 'Bye-bye, baby.' He extends a finger and a tiny fist closes over it, like a mollusc. Jan catches Patrick's eye.

'Look,' she says, 'why don't you stay and have supper?'

As the light fades they carry out dishes and glasses, someone lights candles. The smell of jasmine and nicotiana floods the courtyard, the white blooms glimmering in the dusk. A Beatles song with vaguely ethnic undertones drifts from the big kitchen. The boy is deft and useful, moving chairs, washing lettuce, slicing tomatoes thinly. He advises Jan how to prune a reluctant quince, sympathises with Patrick's classroom work-load. He is curious about the practicalities of obituary-writing, the fact that sometimes they are written before the person has died.

'I think that'd make me feel I was summoning death, maybe hastening the end.'

'Yes, it can be like that. You feel like the executioner's assistant,' Stuart admits.

Patrick looks surprised. 'You've never told me you felt like that about it.'

Marie-Hélène comes out of the house, irritably brushing back her hair. 'No reply from the bloody production office. It's always the same.' The boy pours wine and silently hands her a glass, his manner turning a simple act into a gesture of sympathy. A trace of deep-seated bitterness breaks the surface of social poise and she says, 'It's just not fair on the children.' Adding, with a dry laugh, 'Or on the wife.'

The children, tumbling about on the grass, scream pleasurably when the boy chases them, a ghostly figure, his face gleaming like bone or mother-of-pearl in the dark. Back at the table he turns to Susan, the pale eyes catching the gold of the candle flame and she knows she will find herself telling him about parents prematurely scythed down, and a life lived in the awareness that other people might be kind – in the way Jan and Patrick are kind – but that good behaviour and what used to be called 'good value' constitute part of the protective colouring that ensures survival for those without a nest or burrow to return to.

Jan continues to think of him as The Boy, neither as Nick nor the Niccolò those ambitious parents saddled him with. At thirty she can feel almost maternal towards him. She watches the other two women reacting to his presence: Marie-Hélène, Patrick's old flame, dimmed into the paler glow of friendship, brightening in the presence of a new male; Susan, whom she hardly knows, a woman too young to be so calm, so self-possessed, to have eyes that give nothing away, that render her beauty somehow inert. She is leaning towards the boy now, elbows on the table, murmuring, like someone at confession.

Preparing lunch, earlier, the two women had found themselves alone in the kitchen and Susan stared out of the window at Patrick cradling the baby, rubbing noses, grinning foolishly, while Marie-Hélène, in a deckchair, brushed and replaited her younger child's hair and kissed the thin neck. Susan, suddenly brisk, turned and smiled brightly at Jan, offering to peel potatoes, and nothing was said.

The children have been manoeuvred into their allocated bunk-beds; the baby fed and settled. Supper is slow to end, the red candles guttering, spilling the last of their wax, bleeding down the heavy silver candlesticks. Above the courtyard, bats flitter like velvet cut-outs against the starry sky; fireflies flash electric-blue signals from the bushes, a frog plops loudly into the lily pond. Beyond the garden, night creatures call to one another, or cry out, scuttling, darting, the unseen countryside seething after the torpor of the day. At the table there is stillness. A comfortable silence. Whether it is Jan or Patrick who speaks, or both together, Susan is uncertain, but the thought is shared by them all: no one could be expected to go off into the wilderness at this hour. He must stay the night.

They find him a bed in an unused room and show him where the bathroom is. He insists on clearing the table before they say goodnight. He seems to know where everything goes, has an instinct for drawer and cupboard contents. The perfect guest.

Jan flinches into consciousness, uncertain of the time, suddenly wide awake, heart thumping. Patrick is asleep, moonlight pouring into his open mouth. An owl hoots. Too late, she finds herself filled with a precisely focused terror: they have invited a stranger into the house, some-one they know nothing about. He could be a criminal – arsonist, serial killer, anything – and along the landing is the nursery: images sweep through her – knives, blades, hammers. A skull frail as eggshell. She recalls, suddenly, the way the boy stood, gazing at his shadow, while Patrick talked of Brocken's Spectre and Walpurgis Night; the witches' revels, presided over by their master, Old Nick, Nick Shadow. The air crackles with unseen lightning; the earth splits open like a skull, evil seeps out and engulfs the unwary. They told him so much, uncovered secrets, laying themselves open . . . The sweat chills on her neck. Moving cautiously, she slips out of bed.

She comes out onto the landing and turns towards the nursery and they come face to face at the top of the stairs. She cries out, recoiling from him.

'What –?' Her throat closes in panic.

He smiles apologetically. 'I was thirsty. All that wine. I went to get myself a glass of water.' She sees that he is empty-handed and he answers the unspoken question.

'Drank gallons in the kitchen. Lovely water up here. Well . . . back to bed.' He pauses. 'Goodnight.'

'Goodnight,' she says, and waits till the door closes behind him. She opens the door to the nursery, crosses the room and looks down at the sleeping child, touches the softly pulsing scalp, the hair like corn floss, the fragile bones. She stands, drinking in the milky sweetness of the infant's breath, soothed. She stays a long time by the cot.

She leaves her bedroom door propped open, the landing visible. When she gets back into bed Patrick stirs and mumbles a question. She means only to say she has been checking on the baby, but the fear spills out of her in whispers – 'We know nothing about him –'

'Go back to sleep,' he says, and gathers her into the curve of his body the way she gathers sheets into her, plucked from the clothes line. The warmth of his body, like the sun-warmed sheets, is comforting and, still worrying, she falls asleep.

Next morning she is up early, before the others, getting breakfast together, when the boy appears. As though to make up for her sharpness in the night she offers eggs, bacon, fruit. He shakes his head.

'Thanks but I never have more than a mug of tea.'

'Help yourself.'

She goes out of the room and up the stairs, checking the room he slept in, to find the bed stripped, sheets neatly folded. Quickly she glances into the cupboard, though what she is looking for she could not say. Missing objects, perhaps?

She comes back to find him standing by the kitchen table, gulping a mug of tea. There is an awkwardness, a sense of something wrong, and the lazy ease of the day before has vanished, soured.

'Do let me make you a sandwich –'

'No thanks.'

He turns to the sink and rinses out the mug, swilling away undrunk tea.

'Thanks for letting me stay . . . making me so welcome.' He seems less graceful this morning, almost abrupt. He goes out to the shed and wheels his bike onto the path. She resists an urge to check the silver. She should call him back, the others might want to say goodbye, still full of the rapport of the easy, wine-filled day, the candle-lit amity of the evening. She resents him for breaking into her warm comfortable circle, causing shock, introducing her to fear in the night. She wants him gone. With a huge lift of the heart she watches him freewheel down the hill, out of sight.

Susan, playing the expected part of the good guest, comes into the kitchen carrying the baby, its cheek against hers.

'I changed her nappy –'

Jan takes the child, hugging her fiercely, as though they have been parted for a long time, as though welcoming her home safe from a long journey, and begins to feed her. Tears seep from her closed lids and drip onto the baby's head.

Susan says, cautiously, 'Jan? Is something wrong?'

Already half ashamed of her foolishness, Jan tries to

explain the terror, her fears that the stranger might murder the child, slashing, battering; slaughter them all, set fire to the cottage, rob them –

'But nothing happened.'

'I know. But you feel so vulnerable. Once you have a family, a child.'

The weekend is coming to an end. Patrick and Jan will stay on, for the half-term break. Marie-Hélène's husband is expected within the hour; there has been a phone call.

Stuart and Susan pack their bags and wander round the garden before the drive back to London, he in his MG, she in her Morris Minor. Earlier they walked across the saddle of the valley to the adjoining hillside; there had been an undercurrent they were both aware of. Now he suggests they pace each other back to London, 'stop for a drink halfway'.

She finds it comforting, catching sight of the red MG in her rear mirror, only to have it roar past, a hand waving, then see it again, idling in a lay-by, waiting for her. When they stop for the promised halfway drink, in the amber-lit glow of the pub lounge, the thread of attraction tugs again, and he offers dinner, that night, in London: 'We'll be back in plenty of time.' Pause. 'I want to see you again.' He smiles encouragingly.

The Welsh kitchen that morning, sun already streaming through the window, baby sucking at Jan's bare breast, had been a place rich in domestic detail and intimate ritual, of emotional transactions life had so far denied Susan. She had felt a pang of envy so sharp that she was shaken. But after all, why envy? Why not anticipation? This, like other choices, lay open to her.

And then the woman she had seen as safe, smug even, swaddled in security, had dissolved into tears, torn between mortification and fearful imaginings – You feel so vulnerable, once you have a family. You'll see.

Choice came into it. Susan, troubled, could see that. One path brought warmth, closeness, a pleasant disarray. Fruitfulness. And the constant possibility of loss. The other was a chillier option, more austere; at best, self-contained, calm. At worst, what? No way of knowing.

She considers now where decisions can lead; which route to take. The road forks many times between the Welsh border and the outskirts of London, but halfway there a decision is made, a turning of a different kind taken, one that is to have lasting consequences.

'So,' he asks. 'Shall we meet?'

'I think I'll be going in a different direction,' she says, and a small weight, like a stone, settles somewhere within her.

*

At first it looked the same, unnervingly unchanged. The Welsh hillside, the sprawling cottage, the people, a baby in a basket lying in the shade of an overgrown bush.

But the long-skirted new mother in bare feet had been the baby the last time Susan was here, the doting pair of that long-ago summer now complaisant grandparents, celebrating a thirtieth wedding anniversary. The music pounding from the kitchen was Oasis, though to Susan it sounded not unlike the Beatles.

They reminisced, astonished to realise she had not been to the cottage since –

'Is it really that long! One loses touch . . . We want to hear all your news. What you've been up to . . .' Unspoken questions hovered. Lovers? Husbands? Children?

Susan gave her calm smile.

'Patrick probably told you I took early retirement. I travel a good deal.'

Susan glanced down the track to the lane, empty in the sunlight. The baby in its basket twitched and shifted, starfish hands waving, eyes wide. She reached out tentatively towards it and a small fist fastened damply on a ringless finger.

'I remember it so well,' she said. 'That weekend all those years ago. That boy . . .'

'Boy?' Jan said.

'You remember.' Susan prompted her. 'How fright-ened you were. For the baby. You said, "You feel so vulnerable, once you have a family –"'

'Really?' Jan shook her head. 'Sorry. It's a blank. More wine?'

The Sugar Palace

The Sugar Palace

They swarmed through the piazzas, clogging the narrow streets. Back-packs and bum-bags, trainers and sports-sandals, camcorders and open maps, green *Michelins* and *Rough Guides*. Accents from Milwaukee, Tokyo, Munich, London . . . Clinging like iron-filings to the group tour-leader, following the furled red parasol held aloft, they surged through the Palazzo Ducale promised on the day's itinerary, heading for the room with the three-star Raphael.

Between the ancient towns, in overcrowded railway coaches the two Englishwomen sat squeezed between voluble strangers. Checking the timetables was tantamount to deciphering Linear B. Susan sweated and cursed quietly. Train-hopping round Italy had its drawbacks.

Finally, in Bologna, when their quiet hotel exploded into Activity Fashion Week and the railways declared a one-day strike, Josie made one of her suggestions: why not hire a car, get out of town and continue the rest of the holiday by road? 'Cut our losses, shall we? Mm?'

It was usually Josie who took the decisions that modified existing plans – 'Perhaps the overnight ferry?' Or, 'I thought lunch early today, say twelve-thirty?' The query was rhetorical. Susan, the perfect travelling companion, invariably acquiesced; the question mark went unchallenged.

They were driving through a small town not far from Turin when, up a side-street, Susan caught a glimpse of a big, pale house set back from wrought-iron gates beyond a drive edged with cypresses. She cried out, 'Stop! Stop!'

Josie slammed on the brakes, alarmed. 'What? What is it?'

'That house back there –'

'What?'

'I'm sure I know it.'

'Really? Is it in the book?'

'No, no! Nothing like that.'

Josie frowned. 'Well then –'

Susan got out of the car and crossed the road, blinking in the noonday heat, her eyes scratchy with dust.

This dust was white. The dust she knew as a child had been dun-coloured, lying thickly on the roadside, soft as velvet. At sunset, churned by the wheels of ox-carts, it glowed pink, like cheap face-powder; sunset was called cow-dust hour. In the rainy season it turned to a lake of mud, a slick the consistency of paint that sprayed carts and cars to a uniform clay beige. This dust was white, floating like a wedding veil.

She stood, staring up at the villa with its square tower, its incongruous veranda. It looked empty, the windows shuttered, the steps littered with dried leaves. She heard Josie's brisk, common-sense voice: 'Press on, shall we?' The rhetorical question mark.

Susan said, 'I need a drink.'

There was a café at the crossroads and Josie ordered espresso coffee for them both. Susan kept glancing back at the villa, a memory fluttering like a half-seen movement at the periphery of vision.

'I know that house . . .'

The dust settled, coating her shoes with a fine, even layer, like talcum powder. She reached for a lump of sugar, let it dissolve on her tongue. And everything came into focus. Peliti's restaurant in Delhi, and a house with cypresses and palms where one afternoon, three old people sat, talking about the past –

'It's the Villa Peliti,' she said.

They had told her there were two villas, the other one 'back in Italy'. This was where it had all begun, where young Federico Peliti had changed from sculptor to pastry cook.

That day in Delhi, clinging tightly to her grand-father's hand, she had walked up the drive of the Villa Caragnano, where a tall, grey-haired man waited on the veranda. Not the great Federico, he was history by then, dead more than thirty years before. She was six and it was her birthday: 15 August 1947; a birthday being cele-brated, it seemed, by the whole city, with parades and firecrackers and crowds running through the streets, which surprised her: she had been told she would have no party this year. Was this her party?

No, no, her grandfather said, it was just Independence Day. Susan asked what independence meant.

'It means freedom,' her grandmother said, 'being able to make your own decisions about what you want to do.'

Her grandfather gave a sort of laugh, somewhere between a snort and a bark.

'That remains to be seen.'

'I should like to be independent,' Susan remarked, 'and do whatever I like.'

'Drink your lemonade, it's time we were going,' said her grandmother.

She should have called the ayah to comb out and replait the child's hair; bereavement was no excuse for untidi-ness. But instead she found herself smoothing the fair head in a movement of involuntary affection. The girl was unused to such gestures and looked up, surprised.

Her grandmother rang the bell for the car to be brought round.

They went to tea at the Villa Caragnano, she and her grandparents, and, while she played with glass marbles from an ebony box, shaking them gently so that they chinked one against another, the grown-ups talked over her head.

Crawling under the table after a runaway marble, curtained behind the heavy chenille cloth, she could barely hear the voices, quiet in the dim room, the blinds at the windows keeping out the sun, the overhead fan turning with a soft, steady groan, like the breathing of a rickshaw-wallah as he pulled them along the street.

Susan, hot even in the shade of the café awning, said, 'I don't want this coffee, I want a lemonade,' and saw Josie's look of surprise. 'Are you sure? Tea would be more refreshing in the long run.'

The long run. It sounded so tiring, the long run. She recalled how she had cracked one marble against another that afternoon, viciously, wanting to split the crystal spheres, feeling excluded. The past was always present for old people, the long-ago always there to be summoned up, comfortingly unchanged, the dead alive again. Muffled, in the high-ceilinged room, the voices rose and fell, overlapping as they talked of Signor Peliti, who had begun by sculpting in marble but who built his true fame on foundations of sugar.

It had been considered somewhat un-English for Lord Mayo, newly appointed Viceroy in 1869, to hold a competition for a chef and a pastry cook. A Frenchman might worry about what was placed before him at table, but an Englishman should surely have more important things on his mind. And Federico, the triumphant confectioner, was an unlikely winner: graduate of the Turin School of Art, a sculptor. 'An amateur in the true sense of the word,' the Viceroy explained to his entourage.

Federico arrived in Delhi, bringing with him a vast array of Italian platters and pans and curious utensils designed for the arcane business of working in sugar. He whipped and creamed and baked and chilled; he built gilded Fabergé cages enclosing crystallised fruit, the caramel filigree fine as spiders' webs.

He created weightless structures of pastry and exotic sweetmeats and perilous towers of cream and chocolate. But his masterpieces were the sugar sculptures he created as table decorations: three-masted schooners, white as though frozen in some polar ice-floe; extravagantly detailed flower-pieces coloured from life, monuments and castles towering three feet tall above the table, all carved with delicacy and precision. Perhaps most admired of all was a pink sugar palace with latticed balconies, a blue ornamental pool gleaming in an inner courtyard with lotus blossoms no bigger than cardamom seeds floating on its surface.

Federico loved his work, but what he loved best was the time after the excitement of creation and the applause of diplomats and princes; the dreamlike interlude of stillness when he wandered through the empty rooms, the shelves and tables and floors scrubbed, a smell of wet stone in the air, implements ranged in readiness for the next challenge.

Another banquet behind him, two hundred at table, including several maharajas and a royal guest of honour, Federico could relax, elegant in his velvet smoking jacket and cap with silk tassel. A thickly starred sky and palms tipped with moonlight glimmered beyond the window to the veranda. Time for a cigar, then bed. But tonight the stillness was broken by a sound. Hardly more than a scrape, a sigh, from the next room, but the room should have been empty. He was alone in the house; a thief could have slipped past the *chowkidar* at the gate. There was plenty here to tempt an intruder. He opened the door an inch, and stared, astonished, at a scene of kitchen chaos: heaps of sugar and pots and pans littered the shelves; on the table, an oozing mess unevenly blotched with colour.

And crouched over it a young Indian, one of the kitchen servants, his white clothes streaked with sugar pink.

Federico was at a loss: the boy was a good worker, though required to do little more than scrape down the work surfaces and wash the utensils. 'Ravindra? What is going on here?'

Haltingly, the explanation came out. There was a bride-to-be, a girl much sought-after. Ravi had felt a need to impress. Boasting of his employment with Signor Peliti he had described the sugar sculptures, particularly the pink palace, with such enthusiasm, such detailed vividness that his listeners had gained the impression, the mistaken idea . . .

'You told the family the palace was of your making.'

Silence. A hopeless shrug.

Disaster had followed: 'She said she would much cherish such a palace, it could be a betrothal gift from me to her.'

So he had watched Signor Peliti at work –

'And helped yourself to my stores, it seems –'

, 'No! I brought my own, sahib. I did not steal.' He stared down at the marble slab. 'Perhaps I shall now kill myself. It will be more easy than to see her under such circumstances.' Ravi's slender face had grown gaunt, his eyes dull with despair.

Federico said, 'You will lose the girl if she does not receive this gift?'

'Oh no. The marriage is arranged. But what will be lost is the way she looks at me. With admiration.'

'Is that so important? With everything arranged?'

Ravi said, 'I am loving her. It is not required, but I do.'

He deserved to be punished, of course, but enough time had been wasted here. The boy had learned a lesson; he would let the young fool off with a reprimand and that would be the end of it.

From the depths of Ravi's tunic-clad breast a sound reached Federico's ears, tremulous, repressed, but audible. A sob.

He stubbed out his cigar and stroked his moustache impatiently. He patted the pink splodge. 'Throw this out. And scrape down the marble.' He reached for an apron. 'We have to start from the beginning.'

They set to work, Federico barking orders, Ravi quick to follow. They set sugar and water boiling, added drops of cochineal, the crimson spreading to an even pink. Then, a splash of vinegar and the syrup foamed, seething like lava.

'Now,' said Federico, 'we pour it, so, into the mould and leave it to dry. And then –'

More sugar, this time coloured green, boiled and poured onto the marble, thickening like dough, which they pulled and folded, drawing it out like bright Venetian glass, till it shone with a satin sheen. This was for moulding into leaves and bushes. They made bubble sugar that thinned, brittle and transparent, for the lotus pool, and blow-sugar, a hot, lifeless lump that swelled and glittered as it grew from the mouth of the blow-pipe.

'From a bag of sugar and a litre of water,' Federico murmured, his teeth gritty from the sweet grains, 'you can create – wonders.' The boy listened as he worked. 'It is a passion, sugar. We are artists, in our way. And now,' Federico added, 'I shall rest while you scrub everything clean. Then we have more to do.'

Later, with his narrow blade he gouged and hollowed and trimmed, shaping the slender pillars, whittling the lattice-work windows. While they worked, the moon moved on, the sky paled. By morning, the palace was finished.

In the gloom of the Villa Caragnano the fan turned, groaning softly, and the child beneath the chenille cloth pressed her hot cheeks to the marble floor. The old voices droned on.

'So the boy's honour was saved and he and his betrothed lived happily ever after?'

'As to that, not altogether. When Ravi proudly

carried home the pink sugar palace his father was most displeased: it seems the design was inspired by a Mogul monument, hence Muslim and quite unsuitable for a Hindu betrothal. He slapped Ravi and told him he was a fool. And after marriage the girl emerged as less than ideal, proving to have a temper that was easily aroused and less easily mollified.'

But by then Ravi, too, had developed a passion for sugar sculpture and demonstrated such ability that Federico allowed him to create a viceregal centrepiece unaided.

When Lord Mayo embarked on his next extended tour of duty, Ravi went with him, as Chief Pastry Cook. In the spartan kitchens of up-country *dak* houses, or setting up his stoves under canvas, he produced dazzling examples of his sugary art, and even when they boarded ship and headed out into the Indian Ocean, Ravi each night presented Lord and Lady Mayo and their retinue with sculptures not unworthy of the master.

He was experimenting with a complex set piece when after some days at sea they anchored off the Andaman Islands and the Viceroy was rowed ashore to inspect the British garrison. By the end of the afternoon Ravi, shaking with elation, knew this sculpture was his finest achievement.

Lord Mayo was ready to return to the ship. At the Port

Blair jetty, a boat waited as the Viceroy and his party came down the steep footpath after inspecting the vast, five-tentacled Cellular Jail where convicted murderers transported from the mainland served life sentences. The sun was almost on the horizon, the sky a radiant pink, and the Viceroy stopped to admire the sunset. The entire party paused, their faces turned to the West, the scene bathed in a rosy glow that was rapidly fading to grey. In the waiting boat, the sailors, too, were watching the sun disappear. Only Ravi was watching the Viceroy, waiting to catch his eye. So only he saw the dark figure racing down the path like a shadow, moving so fast that Ravi felt a movement in the air like a wind, a moment before the man leapt on Mayo, clinging to his back like a tiger on its prey, his arm rising and falling. It all happened too fast, and then it was too late. The attacker was wrenched from the Viceroy's back; Mayo staggered slightly. He seemed unhurt. Then slowly he toppled into the water, the sea now too dark for the blood welling from his body to be visible. From the boat Ravi had already dived into the water and he reached Lord Mayo first, holding him above the surface until he was dragged into the boat. Ravi followed, huddled small, shaking. He knew it was too late. The Viceroy would never see his centrepiece, the shoal of flying fish rising from the sea, their curved bodies gleaming silver, fashioned in such a way that, through a trick of the light and the mastery of Ravi's fingers, they seemed to spring free of the foam and hover in the air. Ravi wept, his tears falling onto his sodden uniform, the white streaked with the uneven pink of Mayo's blood.

Josie asked eagerly, 'And what happened next?'

Susan frowned. Happened? Next? She had cried noisily, burying her face in the velvety tablecloth. The old Italian had drawn her out from under the table, contrite for having neglected her, being kind, whispering that it was only natural, 'under the circumstances'. Her grandfather, bracingly, had suggested that the child was probably in need of her tea. Excessive emotion was not something that should be encouraged, and in any case the loss of parents through accident, epidemic or violence was not uncommon in India. He had explained that to the child when it happened to her a few weeks earlier. The birthday party had, needless to say, been cancelled as inappropriate under the circumstances.

Their host had fed her cakes and sugar fruits from one of the Peliti shops and given her chilled boiled milk. After tea he showed her the photograph album, and the picture of Signor Peliti's villa in Caragnano near Turin.

'Perhaps one day you will visit the villa,' he said to the

child. 'When you go Home – (Home? But home was here. Wasn't it?)

She remembered the stiff, smooth board of the photographs, the charcoal-grey roughness of the album pages, the white glare of the villa, bleached by the sunlight. She was accustomed to whiteness: white uniforms, white dhotis, cool white dresses on cool white women. The white of sugar. When people died, violently, in that hot climate, brightness spurted like cochineal, white clothing turned sugar pink –

'Perhaps it's open to the public, your villa,' Josie said, and demanded of the waiter, '*Questa villa, e possibile visitarla?*'

But before he could answer, Susan said, very firmly, 'No.' She glanced at her watch. 'It's too late now. Press on, shall we?' The question mark was rhetorical.

*

Federico Peliti: born Caragnano, Italy, 1844.
Died India, 1914
Lord Mayo: born 1822.
Assassinated Port Blair, 1872

Hortus Inclusus

Hortus Inclusus

The pigeon and the old lady both got on at Kew, the bird
just ahead of her. It waddled across the empty carriage,
searching out fragments of crisp or nut from empty,
discarded packets. Millie settled her bulging plastic
carrier bags on either side of her and watched it without
curiosity. She was used to pigeons on the District Line,
they often nipped on board for a swift snack and hopped
off as the doors were closing. But this time two people
hurrying to catch the train – a young African in a
business suit and a blonde girl in torn jeans – jumping on
at the last minute, got in the way. The pigeon was still on
board as the train moved out.

The girl slumped down near Millie, then a moment
later, got up and moved further away. Millie was used to
this, it happened all the time.

The other two occupants of the carriage eyed the bird
doubtfully. As it fluttered hopefully towards the window, hovered and fell back, defeated by the glass, they
both flinched and the man held his slim, rigid briefcase to
his chest, like a shield.

'It's all right,' Millie said, 'they're quite harmless.'

He looked unconvinced. 'He's just a bit lost,' she added.

He adjusted his dazzling white shirt collar. 'I don't want it dropping anything on my suit.'

'Shitting, you mean?' the blonde said, and laughed. 'Yeah, you'd look a right state.' She added, without force, 'I hate birds. They analysed those pigeons in Trafalgar Square. It was in the papers. They carry disease, pigeons.'

She held up her hands and gazed dreamily at her nails, gleaming talons of dark emerald enamel. They were very long, an inch or more beyond the fingertip, studded with rhinestones, banded with silver filigree and strung with frail silver chains embedded in the enamel surface. They glittered against her white skin like brilliant, elongated beetles. She caught Millie's astonished glance.

'Doesn't it hurt?' the old woman asked.

The girl looked at her pityingly. 'Extensions. Just had it done. Lovely. 'Course I'll be useless for the next two days, forget any washing up.'

'Don't you have to type or anything?' Millie said.

'Off sick, aren't I?' The blonde waved her hands languidly and the beetles flashed silver and green. She yawned.

The pigeon fluttered up towards the window again, banged into the glass and fell back, scrabbling for a moment at the invisible barrier. It hopped a few inches and cocked its head nervously at Millie.

For a moment or two they stared at each other. 'Don't worry,' she said, soothingly, 'we'll be at Gunnersbury any minute. You can get back from there.'

'Does it know how to change platforms?' the girl asked, and laughed again, unkindly.

Millie closed her eyes and thought about her trip to the Royal Botanical Gardens at Kew. Well, not the Gardens as such, it cost even the general public £4.50 just to get in, now, and 'concessions' they'd told her, speaking loudly as though she couldn't hear, were £3. What a joke. In the days when it cost a penny anyone could go in, spend hours wandering. Today she had gone up to the turnstiles and studied the board of rules and regulations for a while. Then she put a question or two: any special opening or closing hours she should know about? That sort of thing. Stared around a bit. Finally she asked if she could go through and just smell one of the flowering shrubs visible a few yards inside, but the attendant said it would get complicated if they started allowing people to pop through just to have a smell, get out of hand. She understood. So she walked back to the Underground station and caught the train. She wished now that the pigeon had waited for the next one.

Flowers were important to Millie. When she went along to the Day Centre she often took a bunch and stuck them in a jam jar; she never stole the flowers, she picked them from building sites or the abandoned gardens of empty houses. Sometimes she had lunch in a deserted garden, she particularly liked the walled ones these Victorian houses went in for, you could prop your back against the warm bricks, get out your sandwiches, no one to bother you. One day she found mint growing by a wall and pushed a few leaves into her bread and cheese. If there was a rosemary bush she rubbed the spiky leaves between her fingers and into her hair, surrounding herself with fragrance. Occasionally there were roses, old, floppy ones. Last week she found a deep red, heavy-headed rose, wrapped close like a cabbage. Ready to drop, it came away in her hand and she sniffed it appreciatively: it smelled, surprisingly, of lychees. She clenched her fist, squeezing the flower hard. She glimpsed crimson between her fingers, like blood. Blood from a rose.

It was flowers, indirectly, that had brought about her friendship with Mrs Marvel, the Monday volunteer helper at the Centre. She had always been very gracious to Millie: 'Do you take sugar? I'll bring it over to you. Call me Josie,' she said, but Millie wouldn't give her the satisfaction. 'Thank you, Mrs Marvel. No sugar.' Then one day Millie went to have a pee and found the elegant helper huddled over the washbasin in tears. Nothing noisy, all very private, but the real thing, the red-eyed, nose-blowing, full works. She straightened up when she saw Millie, apologised and tried to smile. 'Bad day, I'm afraid. It's the anniversary of my husband's death. I thought this year it would be all right, but it catches up with you at the oddest moments. I was doing the cross-word –' Her eyes began to fill again. Millie, for some-thing to say, muttered, 'Well, it's the Chelsea Flower Show next week. That'll cheer you up, won't it?'

Josie was astonished. 'How did you know?'

'I didn't,' Millie said, 'but flowers cheer most people up –'

'I mean that it was the Chelsea Flower Show?'

So Millie had to explain that she knew about horticul-tural matters, kept up a bit. Though the gardening scene was not what it used to be, she disapproved of all these bright colours, she found them quite vulgar; the perfect garden was white, wasn't it? And secret. The enclosed garden.

'Ah,' Josie said, thinking aloud, 'the *hortus inclusus*.'

'That's it.'

Josie said, 'Look: I have two tickets for the show. Would you like to come?'

'Will they let me in?'

'Of course. You'll have a ticket.'

'It won't do. They'll think I pinched it or something. I mean, do I look like someone with a ticket for the Chelsea Flower Show?'

Winter and summer Millie wore a raincoat over a sort of frock and pinafore. The original colours had long ago been superseded by the patina of age, weather, grime, spilled food. Her greying hair could be glimpsed from beneath the brim of a brown felt hat retrieved from a tip. She wore sandals with much-laddered tights, two pairs in winter.

'You'll be with me,' Josie said. There was more she wanted to say, and she cast about for tactful phrases. Then she remembered that her grandfather had been a captain of industry and a blunt man.

'But you do smell,' she said baldly. 'I'd like you to have a bath.'

On the day of the Chelsea Flower Show Millie was collected early from the Centre and taken home by Josie Marvel. She left her plastic carrier bags in the hall and followed Josie to the bathroom.

'Look,' Josie said, 'it's up to you, but I've put out a few things in case you'd like to change . . .' She went out quickly, closing the door behind her.

Millie nosed her way round the room like a dog, sniffing the bath salts, the cluster of shell-shaped soaps in a white porcelain basket, the hand cream and the pot of jasmine growing on the window ledge. The room was wallpapered, flowers climbing to the ceiling. The paintwork shone softly. She turned the taps on and off, crumpled the towels, opened and closed the mirrored cabinet. She stroked the wicker chair, painted white and piled with cushions, and noted that the floor was carpeted. Then she ran the bath.

When she took off her clothes she was startled by the sight of her naked body in the mirror, it was like seeing some strange animal, the skin vaguely blotched and striped, sagging into folds, crinkling like crepe paper. She was shocked by her pubic hair, grown sparse and grey, and got quickly into the deep, foaming bath.

Afterwards, towelling herself dry in something the size of a bed-sheet, she watched the water draining away and saw with some dismay the thick layer of speckled grime that now coated the gleaming enamel. She was reaching for the cleaning liquid when she remembered that she had not asked for any of this and decided that the bath would stay as it was. She wrapped herself in the big towel and sat back in the wicker chair, rubbing her hair dry.

She had been offered a bath once, at Christmas, by

one of those charitable outfits, and accepted, but it was a workaday affair, cracked tiles, stained walls and a dankness in the atmosphere. She was through it in five minutes, and out again, like an old crock in a car wash: clean but hardly sparkling. Here, in the warm, scented air, she moved to a statelier rhythm, she lingered in the brightness.

She emerged from the bathroom wearing the blouse and skirt Josie had put out, plain but good. And the underwear. 'I'll borrow this stuff for the show,' she said. 'It's no skin off my nose and it'll make *you* feel better.'

When they got back, hours later, Josie made them a cup of tea. She was elated, feeling something of a Henry Higgins after Eliza's success at the ball. Millie had been a triumph, debating the subtleties of pruning and propagation, discussing rare plants with one of Josie's friends, the vagaries of fashion with another – 'Don't talk to me about *Corydalis flexuosa*, you see them all over the place. The *cashmeriana*, that's the one to go for. Needs care but worth it. And as for those nasty, chocolate-coloured Cosmos . . .' She sniffed and examined, questioned and compared, her small, lined face growing flushed and moist. On the way home Josie had asked where she learned about horticulture but Millie had shrugged off the question. 'The public library,' she said.

She wandered over to the window and looked down at Josie's tiny, exquisite patio, York-stone underfoot, old walls, a fig tree, a creeper foaming with white blossom like fresh-fallen snow against the dark leaves –

'What do you think of my little *hortus inclusus?*' Josie asked, pouring the tea.

Once Josie had revelled in a garden riotous with hollyhocks and roses, marigolds and golden rod, pink mallow and purple clematis; cornflowers and Canterbury bells. But things change, and her garden changed with her circumstances. The courtyard she had now was white; cool and calm. At dusk, with the blooms shimmering against the ivy and evergreens, it took on the romantic intensity of an operatic grove. Josie had decided that in the long run, horticultural perfection was easier to maintain than happiness.

Millie said, 'Nice. Safe. Secluded. And you're out of the wind.' She gulped down her tea. 'I'll just get my things on and I'll be away.'

'Oh,' Josie said tentatively. 'I didn't want the clothes back – you can keep them, you know.'

'No thanks. I wouldn't feel comfy like this.' Millie plucked at the creamy blouse. 'But I'll keep the knickers.'

She dressed quickly, back turned to the mirror, and tried not to inhale the suddenly unwelcome smell of her own clothes. She decided to pocket a yard or so of toilet paper, she liked the floral border. Too good to use, really.

She collected her plastic bags and nodded briefly to Josie. 'That was nice.'

'Can't I give you a lift somewhere?' Josie asked.

'No point,' Millie said. 'Don't know where I'm heading tonight.'

She hurried away, down the quiet, tree-lined street, up to the main road, and along the shopping arcade. It would be quite a walk but she was used to that. She made it to the river before the tears came, hot, gushing, shaking her like an ague, filling her with an aching remembrance of things lost, of shared moments, of a time when her own body did not disgust her.

'Have you been married?' Josie had asked her, earlier.

'Yes,' Millie said. 'He died.'

He died, killed by something he loved. Who could imagine a rose thorn would carry tetanus, an old rose prove fatal?

Josie, stricken, said, 'I'm sorry.' Before she could stop herself, she was asking, as people had after John's death, 'When did it happen?' As though dating the event somehow defined it.

'Long ago,' Millie said. 'He was a gardener.' At Kew, she could have added, and these days she couldn't even get inside the place.

She found an overhanging shelter near the river and bedded down for the night, the bulging plastic bags creating a barrier against the chill wind and the occasional dog that lifted a leg before passing on.

Bloody Josie Marvel and her bloody *hortus inclusus*. That was what did it. Brought it all back. The Song of Solomon. 'A garden inclosed is my sister, my spouse, a spring shut up, a fountain sealed.' They meant to have a secret garden of their own, one day, but things don't always work out the way you think. She made up her mind to see Kew again, just for old times.

The pigeon had lost interest in food now, all it wanted was to get out of the train. At Gunnersbury it was waiting by the doors, but more people surged in, paying no attention to the bird hopping to and fro, trying to get past them. The doors closed. It began moving nervously about the carriage, flapping anxiously, losing its balance on the ridged floor. Millie took out a leftover bit of sandwich and dropped a few crumbs. The pigeon sidled over and pecked at them. For a moment it seemed calm. Then a sudden panic sent it careening up to the ceiling, crashing into the lights, blundering from one side to the other, shedding feathers.

The other passengers took fright and abandoned the compartment, some shrieking, jostling each other to get out through the connecting door to the next carriage. Millie made cooing noises, drowned out by the sound of the train, which had picked up speed and was rocking along, increasing the pigeon's frenzied need to get free. Crazed with fear, it hurled itself against walls and windows, damaging itself, bleeding, wings broken, blind now to any sense of direction. At last it dropped to the floor almost at her feet, wings outspread as though still in flight, its neck twisted so that it seemed to be staring up at her. Accusingly, Millie thought, but corrected herself: no, that's fanciful. Birds' eyes don't have expression. They're bright. And then they go dull, in death. The pigeon's eyes were now dull. She disliked having it there, at her feet, but found it hard to move, to gather up her heavy plastic bags and step over the small body. So she leaned down and picked up the bird, cradling the battered corpse. She sat there as the train stopped at Turnham Green and Stamford Brook. People hesitated at the doors, saw the pigeon and Millie, frozen, as though sitting for a portrait; a Surrealist composition – *Madonna with Dead Pigeon* – and moved on hastily to the next compartment.

At Ravenscourt Park, three skinheads paused in the open door and surveyed the carriage: the blood and feathers smeared on windows, roof and walls, the white splatter of birdshit on the seats.

'Hey,' one of them said, clearly impressed.

'Yeah.'

They sat down opposite Millie and stared at her. 'Didn't know bag ladies went on trains.'

'Shouldn't be allowed, in my view.'

Millie felt a fluttering begin in her stomach and move up to her throat. Breathing suddenly became difficult. She would never reach the emergency handle in time. This was why she had kept off the trains for so long. She closed her eyes and sat, pressed small in her seat, swaying slightly as the train started. She could hear them talking, perhaps they intended her to.

'Shouldn't be allowed. Dirty old thing like that.'

'Right.'

'Needs to be taught a lesson.'

'Put in her place.'

'Jim?' one of them called above the noise of the train. 'What d'you think? Plenty of time before we get to Hammersmith. Why not, eh?'

She heard the third man's voice through the roaring in her head.

'Nah. Leave her be. She's a nutter, that one. Look what she done to the pigeon.'

A Small Request

A Small Request

Beyond the western outskirts of the city a river wound through the stony landscape like a slow, fat snake. A straggle of makeshift huts edged out from the last streets. Animals, some small, some large, criss-crossed between parched fields and pot-holed tarmac. There were banyan trees and thorn bushes and a shrub that for a brief season brought forth crimson flowers.

On the town side of the river there was a carpet factory. On the opposite bank the brick yard sprawled. Early in the morning the riverside was crowded with children; strangers might have thought they were on their way to school. But these were the workers, gathering. The brick-yard boys worked mostly out of doors, sweating with the heat of the sun and the kiln. The carpet-weavers vanished into their long, dim shed.

Sanjay worked at the yard for a while, but he had a problem with the hot bricks: too often he let them slip through his fingers and they chipped or broke. The boss would admonish him – a yell of rage followed by a swift kick was usual, though Sanjay was fast on his feet and often managed to roll with the blow, even avoid it altogether. The others laughed at him, in particular Alok, the tallest boy, who said the new kid was clumsy and would be better off where he belonged, on his mother's hip.

Nobody understood what Sanjay was doing; that he was carrying out a strategy. The next time he fumbled with the bricks Sanjay explained to the boss that it happened because his hands were too small. He was brushed away irritably, but the boss's brother was there that day and Sanjay held up his hands, flapping them under the man's nose, showing how flexible his fingers were. 'I can bend them right back,' he said, 'I'd be much better at carpets.' The brother owned the carpet factory across the river. 'Nimble fingers,' Sanjay said, 'small knots. Try me.' He crinkled his face into an encouraging smile.

Before the brick yard he had done other jobs: he started out cleaning shoes, his father showing him the way. Sanjay carried the cleaning materials in a small wooden box, and went after tourists or businessmen. 'Clean your shoes, sahib?' He was two when he began, and wobbled as he trotted after them, unsteady on his feet, but the men liked him, the chubby infant looked appealing with his hopeful grin, tugging at jacket or shirt until they allowed him access to their shoes. He picked up some English from the tourists, and the childish lisping of the phrases made the businessmen laugh. Holding their gleaming briefcases over his head, they warned him, genially, to make sure the polishing brush did not so much as nudge their immaculate trousers if he valued his life. Things were going well. Then one rainy season the family got washed out, the roof of the hut collapsed and they needed somewhere new to sleep.

There was a *bustee* on the other side of town that Sanjay's mother had seen once: the unpaved dirt-road, bordered with makeshift huts, had the luxury of two water taps. An open drain ran down the middle of the road. From the huts, electric flexes could be – discreetly, and of course illegally – connected to the electricity supply. To Sanjay's parents it was a residence they could hardly aspire to. There was an empty spot. They could have moved in, put up a roof. But there was a problem, a man who had to be sweetened; new arrivals neglecting to offer the necessary tribute could find their roof stamped flat next day.

Sanjay's family had nothing to offer.

The man in charge said he sympathised with their situation, he would like to help. He told Sanjay's father about this friend of his, with the brick yard. It meant Sanjay would no longer be living at home, and his mother was uneasy. 'Pulling hot bricks out of the kiln, isn't it painful?' But the man said not at all, cooling procedures were well looked after. And in any case – 'How old is the boy? Eight? He'll be put with the women, shaping the clay for the bricks. Easy work.' And he added that there would be no problem finding Sanjay's family a corner in the *bustee*; in fact he had a few bits of tin for a roof they could have for nothing. So they agreed and Sanjay's father shook hands on it. They moved into the settlement and he gave them a small down-payment which guaranteed the boy would be employed for five years. 'Regard it as an advance against earnings,' he said. The child would work it off in time, though of course his food and keep would be deducted.

Next day he collected Sanjay to drive him to the brick yard. Sanjay sat in the back of the truck and as they went off saw his mother's blank face, the youngest on her hip, the other two little ones staring, the older one carrying the shoe-cleaning box that had been Sanjay's. The man with influence waved out of the window of the truck and called out that the boy would be all right. 'Mothers worry too much!' he shouted.

Sanjay slept in an open-sided hut at the yard. He soon got the hang of shaping the bricks: scooping the clay, filling and levelling off the moulds. The clay made mysterious sucking noises as he worked it; soft, smooth, a pale greyish colour, like his mother's skin in the light just before dawn. When the bricks were dry they carried three or four at a time to stack them for firing, which he managed quite well by balancing them across his forearms. He was settling in, but after a while he was put on the kiln. This was less agreeable, especially when it got so hot that he had to keep hopping like a monkey to stop his skin blistering. He hopped as fast as anyone but the bricks fell from his hands rather too often. The others, of course, simply thought he was clumsy. Alok said he was useless, and should be chucked into the river like the kittens they sometimes caught, no one would miss him and there would be more food to go round. Occasionally, hopping and dancing on the burning surface of the kiln, Sanjay dreamt briefly about his mother's food, the miracles she could achieve out of a handful of flour and some withered vegetables, and his mouth watered.

Twice a day they saw the boys from the carpet factory in the distance. The looms made a humming sound like angry bees that could be heard right across the river, but there was never any shouting or calling out; the boys came out, blinking in the sunshine and stretching slowly, like stray dogs. Half an hour later they were back inside.

Sanjay, watching them as he danced and burned, saw that life was different, quieter, across the river, and one day, when they were prevented from shaping bricks because of the rain pouring down, washing everything away so that even Sanjay had nothing to do except stand there, dripping, he thought how nice and dry the carpet factory must be on such a day and he made his long-planned move. He went up to the boss who was talking to his brother, and waggled his hands in their faces. 'Nimble fingers,' he said, his face crinkling into the practised grin.

It was always dark in the carpet factory; the boss had his reasons for this: 'They work by feel anyway, so what's the point of wasting electricity?' Sanjay understood now why the boys stood blinking in the sunlight when they came out. He blinked, too, because the light hurt his eyes. But life was certainly quieter here, he had been right about that. They worked at the looms in silence. This was another of the boss's rules. He said it helped concentration.

Every now and then the factory had some visitors, people who looked over the place and made notes. They would ask questions, and watch the boys working and when they asked why everyone was so quiet the boss explained that the workers were concentrating: 'If they are chatting around they make errors and this is expensive.' He did not add that it was expensive only for the workers, because mistakes were always charged to the boy concerned. One visitor asked why the windows were not open, and he flung up his arms in frustration: 'Evil insects fly in, and consume the fabric of the carpets. Also, pollution is a great problem here. Dust from the brick works.' Sanjay was unsure about the dust, but the carpet fibres certainly floated in the air, he could see them, like pale, lazy mosquitoes drifting past. They got in his throat and made him cough and there was nowhere to spit so he had to swallow them.

The day the two Englishwomen called in, things had been going badly for him already: as he had anticipated, nimble fingers were fine for doing the tiny knots and keeping the texture smooth, but he had to pull evenly on the thread and keep his hands bent in a certain position to handle the loom, and that day one of his calluses started bleeding and some of the blood dropped onto the carpet and might have stained the pattern. This could have earned him a crack round the head, but the boss was busy welcoming the visitors, two women from some foreign outfit, who wanted to see how the factory operated. They walked round, asking the usual questions. Sanjay prayed fervently to Ganesh for the day to go well. Elephant-headed Ganesh was an amiable god, he loved laughter and merriment, and, having four arms and a trunk, would have been particularly skilled at carpet-weaving, had it ever proved necessary. Praying to Ganesh, Sanjay asked not for any special favour or personal gain; merely for a good day that ended well.

The visiting women were old, about his mother's age, and dressed in locally made garments which they must have bought in town: brightly coloured cotton tunics and trousers, unflattering to their English colouring. One was thin, with sharp bones in her face, the other had hair the colour of ashes and a thick waist. Sanjay thought they looked ugly, but friendly. As they walked round, some of the boys called out, in English, 'What is your name?' One of the women said her name was Susan and asked the nearest worker, 'And what is *your* name?' The boy, who knew only that one sentence himself, burst into giggles, repeating again and again, 'What is your name!' until the visitor moved on. The women studied work in progress and asked questions in English. A local man translated them, and the boys' answers. Sanjay was puzzled by some of the questions: how many rest periods and days off the boys had and how often they saw their families. He still remembered a bit of English from the shoe-cleaning days, and when the Susan lady got to him and put a question about how long they worked each day, he replied, 'Twelve hours,' in English. Her eyes opened very wide and the boss quickly said to her that the boy had misunderstood the question.

She took one of Sanjay's hands in hers, which meant he had to stop working the loom. He looked down at her soft, pinkish paws, aware she was lightly stroking his scarred fingers, like someone soothing a very tiny bird, and then she held out the boy's bleeding hand to the boss and asked another question.

The boss said, laughing and waving his arms about, 'Boys, madam, are being boys!'

Sanjay's vocabulary wasn't up to the next bit, but he did pick up something about playing rough games outside on stony ground. Then the woman asked about food, and Sanjay said it was 'OK', another word he remembered. He could see the boss behind her giving him the familiar look. But then she said, 'Are you ever hungry?' which he understood immediately, from the old days, going up to businessmen, calling out 'Hungry boy! Clean your shoes, sahib!' and he knew he should say no but he found he was nodding and saying, 'Yes.'

She turned to the boss and there was a conversation for a minute or two. Then he shrugged irritably and called out, 'The ladies are bringing in some food tomorrow. I have explained that there is no need, but they insist. It will give them pleasure, so we will all enjoy an extra break, for special refreshments.'

Nobody said anything, and the two went off waving goodbye at the boys. Sanjay wondered what they would bring, maybe sweetmeats, or cakes – Englishwomen were always eating cakes, everyone knew that. But when they arrived next day with a van from town they brought real, serious food. Someone had given them advice.

The plump one spoke to Sanjay: she knew he understood English. 'Today is a special day for us, a festival we celebrate every year,' and she showed him a coloured picture of some people sitting in an open-sided hut which Sanjay thought looked very like the one he now slept in, but surrounded by a landscape that could only have been dreamed up by the man who made the painting: bright green fields folded round small, soft hills, spiked with dark trees like pointed brushes. The picture showed an old man and a mother and baby and three servants carrying silver dishes of food, but Sanjay saw at once that this must be a gathering of deities: one a donkey, another a sheep, and a winged incarnation hovering overhead. A couple of sacred cows looked on placidly. The woman put the picture away in her bag and said, 'Of course, I know you have your own gods.'

It was time to eat. The boys left the machines and lined up: there were lentils and brinjal, potatoes and rotis, and Sanjay sat by the door, in the shade, feeling the breeze, and ate slowly, licking his fingers and the plate, saving the best bits till last. The women walked around looking pleased and the boss thanked them both, bowing and grinning cheerfully. He came up to Sanjay and patted the boy's head quite hard, and said, without raising his voice, still beaming, 'Tomorrow you'll all work an extra half-hour to make up for time lost today.' He gave Sanjay his long look and added: 'Plus major financial deduction for you, this being your fault for answering questions without due care.'

From the brick yard across the river Sanjay heard the shouts and yells of the boys, and once or twice a howl that indicated a new boy, unprepared for burned feet, had stepped onto the kiln. He heard Alok, heard his special, rasping shout, cursing as he lifted the hot bricks. Alok was probably weeping silently, he often did, while he cursed and flinched, the skin of his face so hot that the tears dried as they fell from his eyes.

Sanjay scooped up the last few scraps on the plate, the cumin potato melting on his tongue. The breeze touched his head, soft as a breath. A good day, ending well.

Trapped

———————

Trapped

The house smelled musty. Empty for little more than two weeks, already it had lost the familiar, year-round emanations that made it theirs: the tang of herbs chopped in the kitchen, the fragrance of the lilies in a tall vase wafting through the hall; a faint, ghostly hangover from washing machine and bath cleaner. Gerald began to open windows.

It was Anna who found the evidence of mice in the larder. She opened the door, gave a scream of horror and backed off, rigid with distaste verging on panic, registering the trail of tiny black droppings on the white shelves, the rice and pearl barley packets raided, invaded, spilling to the floor. A yellow pool of liquid gleamed dully from a nest of plastic shopping bags.

'God! They've peed all over the place, I can't cope with this.'

Gerald took over. He threw out the spilt pulses and stained plastic bags and cleaned the shelves. Never had holiday euphoria evaporated quite so quickly. Five hours ago they had been sipping white wine under an Italian arcade, feeding each other green and black olives, and here he was, on his knees, clearing out mouse droppings.

Coming home was always difficult. 'The re-entry problem,' Gerald called it, jokily, a convenient umbrella to cover a general, unspecified disquietude; perhaps no more than the tension between the drag of urban gravity and the weightlessness of Abroad.

'The yellow stuff's not urine, by the way,' he called. It was brine, leaking from a plastic container of olives – the mice had chewed efficiently through the packaging, before deciding they did not care for the taste.

An hour later the larder was pristine.

'They'll come back,' Anna said.

'Probably not. The house was empty, remember. They'll be too scared, now, with us tramping about the place.'

She gave him a sceptical look. 'I bet they come back.'

Next morning, the tiny seeds of doom were scattered over shelves and floor, and Anna made it clear she expected Gerald to do something. 'Set a trap. Whatever.'

He knew they must get rid of the mice, of course. But he could not bring himself to do the deed. What then? There was no way he could call in the Council: a few droppings hardly constituted an infestation. Fumigation was for bugs and fleas. What did people do about mice, squeamish people, infirm of purpose? Wasn't there a humane alternative to assassination? Of course there was the cat option, but that was out, too. Anna didn't want animals, or ties of any sort. They had talked about all that sort of thing, early on, in one of those conversations about plans for the future.

'You don't mind, do you?' She had looked at him questioningly. 'It's perfect, just the two of us, don't you think?'

'Perfect,' he said, waiting for her smile of relief.

Gerald liked their house with its high ceilings and long, walled garden, but sometimes he felt oppressed by it: behind the sparkling paintwork of the doors, the emptiness of rooms hummed at him. He thought it was too big if it really was to be just the two of them. He had said so, to Anna one day, but it was a conversation that led nowhere. Or rather, that led, guided by Anna, to a discussion of where they might go next: Greece? Portugal? Island hopping? 'We're free as air,' she said. 'Aren't we?'

'Free as air,' he agreed.

On the way to the station, deep in thought, he bumped into a neighbour.

'Sorry, Susan. I was miles away.'

'Evidently. Nice holiday?'

They fell into step together. Susan was fifty-something; closer to his mother's generation, she had that jam-making, church fund-raising competence. His mother, picking runner beans or dead-heading roses, had the same unhurried rhythm. Susan had invited Anna and Gerald to tea, once, when they moved in. Anna had been delayed by a transatlantic telephone call from a colleague and Gerald had arrived alone. Sitting in Susan's shady garden, the teaspoon tinkling against the eggshell-thin cup, he was suddenly overwhelmed by a childhood memory of similar moments; the cosiness, the certainty that homemade cake was on its way and nothing nasty lurked behind the bushes.

There was something about Susan's calm, incurious gaze, her comfortable body, that caused him now, to his own surprise, to spell out his dilemma: his unwillingness to harm the small intruders.

She recognised the problem immediately. In India, she said, where she had lived for a while, dangerous snakes flourished. But there were natives who, far from killing them, worshipped the snakes and left offerings of food, for example in bamboo groves where cobras dwelt.

'They sometimes left saucers of milk outside windows.'

'I thought that was to keep away the elephants,' Gerald said and had his levity rewarded by a blank look. Good woman, Susan, but not strong in the humour department. Still, she gave him the solution: for people who found killing unacceptable, there was a trap that was just that and no more, a prison in which the captured mouse sat waiting until released.

The hardware shop had three on view and Gerald chose the one made of wood because it looked less grim – a sentimental touch, he acknowledged ruefully: choose pine for your mouse-trap to go with your country-kitchen cupboards . . .

Next morning when he peered into the larder, the cage held a small, furry prisoner. Triumphantly he carried it to the end of the garden and released the occupant.

Anna cleaned out the larder, scrubbed shelves, replenished tainted stores and relaxed.

Two days later she recoiled from tell-tale signs in the butter: toothmarks like tiny furrows.

Again Gerald set the trap, and again released his prisoner. The following day the signs were there in plenty. 'God, there must be a whole flock or herd or tribe of the things.' She sounded distraught. 'You've go to *do* something.'

'I will,' he promised. 'Leave it to me.'

Promises were easily made, less easily kept. Next morning, going through the now-familiar routine, Gerald picked up the cage and looked closely at the mouse. He wondered whether in fact it might be the *same* mouse, coming back for more. Could this be a one-mouse operation? A lone ranger? As an experiment, he decided to tag the creature, the way ornithologists do with migrating birds. He put the cage in the garage and waited for Anna to go for her daily jog in the park.

He watched her from the bedroom window, trim in her running gear; the slender ankles, the tender hollows of her neck; and as she looked left and right, crossing the road, trainers rhythmically pounding the tarmac, he caught the look of determination, the concentration in her small, pale face and, as always, his heart seemed to shift, contract, and he felt close to tears. From afar she looked so small. Almost a child.

He found her nail scissors and went out to the garage. The mouse felt warm in his hand, vibrating with frustrated movement, the heartbeat fast, fluttering. He marvelled at the way the fur fitted so neatly, like a glove, no sags, no leftover bits. Beneath the flesh he could feel the fragile bones, a whole geometry of skeletal interconnection. Gently he drew one tiny paw away from the body and trimmed off a line of fur, a sort of bracelet, an identity marker. Then he carried it outside and let it go. Next day he checked the captive: it was the same mouse.

Trapped

They looked at each other. He was convinced the mouse was pleased to see him, but this time, thinking of Anna, he walked to the very end of the garden, leaned over the creeper-clad brick wall and set it free in the long grass leading up to an unoccupied house. He scattered a few bits of cheese ahead of the released prisoner: survival rations, and also, in the manner of a paper-chase trail, to lead it away, to new territory.

But he set the trap again, and wondered how long it would take, this time. Because he knew now that the mouse was not going away. He contemplated a name for it. Names were important.

When it returned, he kept the news to himself. He thought about building a mouse-run, establishing the occupant in its own comfortable setting, with somewhere warm for the winter, maybe finding it a companion. But the logical extension to that would be mouselets, minute, pink, naked babies that squirmed, blindly seeking nourishment, dependent, vulnerable. Messy. And Anna disliked mess. So: a solitary then. But there was no reason, was there, why the mouse couldn't be made comfortable; live in luxury, well-fed, in congenial surroundings? It would simply have to adapt to its condition.

No, Gerald thought. And let it go.

But the mouse kept coming back.

He tried to keep it from her by getting up early, speeding the release and cleaning out any droppings, and for a while the ploy succeeded, but one morning she caught him.

Anna's delicately balanced equilibrium nose-dived. 'Mice are disgusting! Disgusting!' she said fiercely. She raged about the house, slamming doors, and rushed off to work in tears, late for a meeting. Gerald recalled her description, soon after they met, of her 'tragic' childhood (it was one of her words, as in tragic haircut or tragic quiche: reductive, dismissive, jokey). She had described her mother's cramped flat, the claustrophobic closeness of so-called family life: the squabbling, the dirty dishes piling up on every surface, the unwashed nappies of younger siblings sending an ammoniac signal from the cluttered bathroom.

'If we'd been a café they'd have shut us down,' she had said to Gerald that day; 'cockroaches were my television: I watched them come and go, pick up their groceries from our kitchen. One day my baby brother tried to eat one. He didn't have enough teeth so it just wriggled out. And as for the mice . . . I don't want to think about it.'

'This can't go on,' she said, when she came home that

night. Gerald promised to search for the tiny mouse-hole which must still exist. He would buy some Polyfilla; block the entry. Establish a mouse-free zone.

They went out to dinner at a new restaurant; one of their better evenings: the music and the clientele were loud and cheerful, the food layered vertically, modishly precarious. They drank a lot, laughed a lot, came home and made love. Next morning, Gerald overslept and she was up before him. He was blearily dragging on his dressing gown when she told him she had bought a proper mouse-trap, one that would administer the *coup de grâce* on the spot.

'Well perhaps that won't be necessary, when I've blocked the hole –'

'I've already set it.'

'Already? You must have been up early.'

He was halfway out of the room when she said, 'I set it last night.'

Gerald went down the stairs quite slowly. Well, no need to hurry, now.

When he opened the larder door relief flooded into him: there was no trap sitting in the usual place on the floor, neither his nor Anna's new one. Then he saw, about a foot away, a steel trap, overturned, a trap that must have leaped in the air when set off, and come clattering to rest, upside down. He reached for it, feeling oddly tired. The mouse was there all right, spine smashed by the powerful spring, stretched out, quite stiff, as though caught in mid-leap, paws splayed. There had been some bleeding, not a lot. A spot, like a tiny scarlet bead, clung to one corner of the open mouth. He touched the pale fur bracelet.

'Well?' Anna's voice floated down. 'Did it work?'

'Oh yes.'

'Just chuck it in the bin, wrap it in a plastic bag.' She remained upstairs, unwilling – or unable – to face the event at close quarters. He picked up the trap: his hand brushed the body and he felt momentarily repelled.

He carried trap and mouse out to the garden and buried it out of sight, behind the lilac bush where the earth was soft.

Gerald spent a long time in the shower, and told Anna not to bother with breakfast.

The train was crowded, stifling. Sealed windows, non-functioning ventilation and air that grew rancid as the passengers swayed together, hip to hip. He felt trapped, and got out a stop early, walking the rest of the way to the office. In the window of a gift shop on the corner, alongside the wooden tulips and the incense holders, he noticed a small display: 'The Perfect Pet for Busy People'. A stone in a stripy box; a large, smooth pebble. 'Keep it on your Desk. Stroke it. Your Quiet

Companion.' He looked at the stone pets in their cardboard boxes and thought, for a moment, about buying one. Then he walked on, to the office.

False Pretences

False Pretences

'How did you meet?' people often asked. They were an odd couple: he fifty-something, with a fondness for cavalry twill and quiet sports jackets; she twenty-one, with fluorescent orange hair and a jewel in her nose. Usually they shrugged off the question with a joke, but once, alone with old friends, she said, 'We met in the street. He was pissing against the wall and I came by and we got talking, the way anyone would, right? And it went on from there.' They all laughed and accepted that Flora was not about to tell them the truth. But in fact, that was exactly how they met.

Matthew being a movie freak (as Flora called it) or a film buff (which was how he would have described the condition) told her their first encounter was a sort of alternative Hollywood moment; a 'cute-meet', as filmed by say, the Coen brothers or David Mamet.

'Naah,' said Flora, still afflicted with vestigial guilt for St Paul's and Oxford, 'it was a straight-up case of mistaken identity. You got me by false pretences.'

'False pretences. Isn't that a tautology? Pretences, by definition, are false. So . . . that would mean *false* pretences are in fact –'

'How about some tea?' she suggested.

'Earl Grey? Lapsang Souchong?'

'Builders,' she said firmly.

They met on Christmas Day. She had spent the morning helping her mother serve turkey, stuffing and veg followed by Christmas pudding, to forty homeless persons in a crypt – not something she particularly enjoyed, but the tradition stemmed from her schooldays and was hard to break. 'A real dose of the *Little Women* crap,' Flora called it. 'You know the way they were always visiting the sick and giving away their dinner to the poor, and all that.' Doing it was a donation to her mother's sense of well-being.

The crypt was dark and smelled of sweat and stale cigarette smoke. Once, long ago, someone had painted the raw bricks with glossy white paint, much of which had flaked off. What remained, grey and sweating with condensation, caught the light with a chilly gleam. Tinsel and flimsy paperchain decorations drooping from the corners of the ceiling to the dusty central light flex merely accentuated the dreariness of the ancient basement. But the mood was determinedly cheerful – until one of the regulars, lining up for food, still wrapped in her balding fun-fur jacket and track-suit bottoms, reacted irritably to the No Alcohol rule. 'A can of bloody lager wouldn't give the Virgin Mary a miscarriage, would it?' she snapped, and told the volunteers they could stuff their turkey where it would give them maximum satisfaction. Then she knocked the can of orange sparkler off her tray. It rolled along the counter like a hand grenade and crashed to the floor. There was a pause, a moment when the whole harmonious fiction trembled on the verge of disintegration. Ladle poised in mid-air, Flora briskly told the woman she was a stupid cow and needed sorting. There was an exchange of looks. Then they both began to laugh.

'Kids today,' the woman said without rancour. 'No bleeding respect.'

She collected her turkey lunch and sat down at one of the trestle tables. Flora called after her, 'You're dead right about the orange fizz – it's filthy muck.'

She went on dishing out the Christmas fare, intrigued as she always was by the variousness of humanity confronting her. There were the literally homeless, fuzzy-faced and ripely unwashed, who kept their coats on and requested second helpings, which were tucked away in pockets for the next day. Then there was the quiet-desperation contingent, the ones Flora thought of as the hopeless cases, respectably dressed, shirts clean, ragged sleeve-edges neatly trimmed with nail scissors. Men most often, depressives, or victims of redundancy or bad divorce, issuing from bedsit or hostel for a few hours of company and warmth.

Someone began to play the battered, out-of-tune piano and the pool table was cleared for action. Flora scrubbed out the last of the dishes, grabbed her jacket and ran up the stone steps into the cold fresh air. She had done her good works stint: now she was heading for a party. The light was already thickening into early dusk. She turned into a narrow, quiet street which would take her up to the main road and her destination. At the top of the deserted street she saw a nondescript male figure turn to the wall and unbutton his overcoat. A moment later a jet of urine arched its way to the bricks. Flora's first thought was: why didn't he do it at the Centre? This was obviously one of her mother's hopeless lunchers, heading nowhere in particular, full of his turkey and two veg, and bursting with orange drink.

She slowed her steps and studied the houses on either side with interest but the steady jet was still splashing the wall. At last, when she was no more than a few yards away, the man went through that instinctive shake-and-adjust thing all men did, and strode towards her. She registered the neat camel overcoat and woollen scarf. Not one of the sleeping-rough homeless: just another hopeless case. To her astonishment, before they drew level, he spoke.

'I really must apologise. I have a problem and there doesn't seem to be a public lavatory in the entire neighbourhood.'

Startled, Flora found herself explaining. 'They've closed them all down. Blame the government. Not cost-efficient.' She noted as he passed her that he had a pale oval face, features of regularity and grace and that his voice was beautiful. What had he been, she wondered, before he fell into the abyss? Her mother had told her of bank managers, advertising men, property-owners, Volvo drivers, whose lives spun out of control and who one day found themselves lining up for a mug of tea at the Day Centre.

Impetuously, Flora turned and called after him, 'The public library's got a loo in case of emergencies. Not a lot of people know that.'

He turned and she smiled at him, over her shoulder, the orange hair like a flame in the deep blue of the dusk.

The party was not a success. Everyone else was three hours and several glasses ahead of her in the happiness mode. She felt bored and wandered into the kitchen for some fresh air. A woman in a sort of Indian nightie asked if she would like to help clear the table, and Flora thought: there's always some loser who ends up at the sink washing glasses. She was backing away when one of the more laddish guests blocked the doorway and clamped her by the shoulder, leaning against her for support.

'Fancy a shag?'

'No thanks,' Flora said. 'I'm washing these glasses.'

It was well into January before she called in at the library to borrow a video. She walked in and there he was: the man with the bladder problem. She recognised him at once: the pale oval face, the dark, panda-like eyes. She wondered if she should say hallo – he might have forgotten their encounter or, if not, be embarrassed. But he spoke first, and again she registered the voice: engaging, attractive, amused.

She was astonished by the coincidence of their meeting: she did not often visit the library. He did not choose to explain he had haunted the place since it reopened after Christmas in the hope of seeing her.

He invited her for a coffee, and she accepted, 'so long as it's my treat'. As they settled themselves at the table she accidentally brushed his coat with her hand. Surprised, she reached out and stroked the surface gently.

'Hey, fantastic. Like velvet.'

'Cashmere. A weakness of mine.'

'So how d'you get a cashmere coat?'

He raised his eyebrows. 'You buy it in Burlington Street.'

For the first time she looked at him properly, at the scarf (probably cashmere too), at the fine shoes, the double cuffs of the shirt –

'You're not a hopeless case at all!' She felt cheated, let down.

'Well, I never said I was. I have a problem, but it isn't hopeless.'

'No, I mean –' She stopped. The explanation was not simple. She shook her head and tried to reach her cappuccino through the froth. She was aware he was looking at her.

Matthew studied her clothes with interest: the too-short sweater with sleeves to her knuckles, the pelmet skirt and man's jacket.

'Where did you get yours – the jacket and stuff?'

'Oxfam.'

'Ah,' he said, nodding. 'Things are certainly tough for young people. Benefit cuts and –'

She said, lethally sweet, 'I have a job in a Cork Street gallery. I dress like this on my day off because I want to. We're not all fashion victims.'

And now it was his turn to feel cheated.

They stayed in the café until it closed, moved to a pub, then onto dinner. Noting how she picked languidly at a salad, he was already worrying about her, aware of the ethereal slenderness, almost hollow-boned, like a bird

you could crush if you handled it carelessly. Too thin.
Fragile.

She was aware he was looking at her.

'What?'

He knew he must watch his words. He picked up her
hand, held it in his, as though weighing it. 'You're as
light as a leprechaun. A goblin.'

'Is that a compliment? It doesn't sound like one.'

They played the 'Anything to Declare?' game: a
painful divorce on his side, a dead father on hers. He
looked surprised. 'He must have been very young –'

'One of those heart things.' She shrugged, heading
off questions. 'It happens.'

They lingered over their coffee until the Italian
waiters, tired-eyed, allowed their professional ebul-
lience to droop and began clearing the room round
their table.

When they came out of the restaurant it was nearly
two and Matthew called a taxi. 'I'll drop you home.' But
they both knew he would give the driver his own
address.

She knew already that he was a literary agent, disen-
chanted by market-led publishing and, as a consequence,
semi-retired. He opened his front door.

'I chucked the office. This is where I live and work,
now.'

False Pretences

She glanced round the Chelsea flat: 'Not exactly a garret, is it?'

Thanks to the estate of an enduringly popular dead author and a slim volume that had stayed on the best-seller lists for years, he was, he confessed, 'indecently solvent'.

Next day he took her to Harrods and bought minia-ture tomatoes, finger-sized carrots, a cauliflower no big-ger than an apple, and cooked her a doll's portion; food for a goblin, he called it. She was amused but did little more than nibble at the food.

He suggested lunch in Paris. They glided through the countryside, sipping champagne, the wintry sunlight showing up the smears on the Eurostar windows.

'Do you do *everything* first class?' she asked, suddenly irritable.

'I'm too old for pigging it.'

'You're not old, you're just a wimp.'

'Isn't that another word for a New Man?'

'Oh, you're definitely too old to be one of those,' she assured him.

One Sunday night she hauled him off to an over-crowded, cavernous dump in Camden Town where the decibels rattled the light fittings and sent tremors through the soles of his feet like vibrations from the engines of an ocean liner. And, as at sea, he began to feel faintly sick, his head buzzing, his mouth dry. Young people, shouting to one another, bumped into him and failed to apologise.

Why is she doing this? he wondered. He knew she was unhappy, the long, slender face closed up, unreadable. She let him suffer for an hour before she relented and they left.

Then, suddenly, there were no more tests, no silent challenges. The next time she went back to her place it was to clear her room and explain the situation to her flatmate.

Flora never told her mother how she and Matthew met – by then there were other problems to be dealt with.

'Old enough to be your father! In fact your father would have been younger, if he'd lived!'

'It doesn't bother me –'

'Not now. But what about later? You'll still be young when he's an old man; and sex doesn't last for ever, you know. What about companionship, the things you do together when you're both over the hill?'

'Well of course you're the expert on that,' Flora said brutally. 'What were you when Dad copped it? Thirty-eight? You really did the smart thing, didn't you?'

A few months later, Flora rang one evening to tell her

mother she and Matthew were married. To her surprise, Josie reacted with anger.

'Typically inconsiderate. I thought at least I would attend your wedding, if and when.'

'But you didn't want me to marry him!' Flora protested.

'No. And obviously I would have preferred someone else. But if it was unavoidable, the least you could have done was to think of others besides yourself.'

'What?' Flora squawked. 'You're being well logical there, aren't you?'

'Please try and speak proper English,' Josie said bitterly. 'God knows I spent enough having you taught.'

'So you won't be wanting a piece of the cake then.'

'Did you *have* a cake?'

'Don't be daft. That was irony.'

Gradually the day-glo orange hair faded to caramel and back to its own wheat-pale blonde. The nose decoration was replaced by a discreet gold stud. Still, there were moments when the generation gap yawned between them; cultural references not picked up – 'Lennie Who?' The only Bruce she knew was Springsteen – resistance when he tried to open doors for her; real doors, to restaurants, hotels, shops – something she learned to tolerate; and portals of another sort, windows onto what he referred to as 'perilous seas' and 'faery lands forlorn', which she described mockingly as the stuff inside his head, debunking his romantic tendencies.

But Flora made him happy. Working at his desk he would catch sight of her drifting past the open study door, coffee mug in hand, her slenderness barely breaking the stream of light from the big window beyond. She lingered in deep baths fragrant with sandalwood and oil of bergamot, and occasionally he stretched out on the carpet, whisky tumbler on his chest, and they talked, breathing the steamy, scented air, the cascading leaves from hanging baskets shading the bath, her body melting into the green-tinted water, mysterious beneath its glowing surface. When she sat up, frail shoulders and breasts gleaming, the wet spiky hair mingled with the hanging ivy and she looked pagan, the long eyes gazing inwards like a Siamese cat's, or those on an Egyptian fresco. Enveloping her nakedness in a bath towel, sleeking her skin with unguents, he anointed a chosen goddess, benign, demanding no tribute.

He bought delicate Japanese tit-bits that gleamed on the dark table, brilliant as jewels, drove to the coast for freshly-caught fish, presented her with hand-made pasta laced with saffron and truffles, biscuits flavoured with champagne, all in the cause of encouraging her fugitive appetite. Without actually raising the subject.

She was less circumspect.

'So what's this problem of yours?' she asked.

'Very unromantic, I'm afraid. A prostate thing. It comes and goes.'

'Is it curable?'

'I believe so.' He was embarrassed, reluctant to discuss something so detumescent-making in its implications.

Flora swept all that aside. She hauled him off to Harley Street, arranged the consultations, booked the hospital. On principle, of course, she was against private medicine, but Matthew was of a different generation, a different mindset, and she no longer felt she wanted to fight that battle. The operation worked, and the problem became a thing of the past. As their first Christmas together approached, Flora told him she wanted to help her mother serve turkey to the homeless and the hopeless cases – 'She hasn't asked, but . . .'

'I'll collect you afterwards,' he offered. She had a better idea.

'Why don't we meet in that street where I first saw you? It'll be a movie moment.'

The day was a success: Flora insisted on importing some good apple juice as a change from the orange fizz, and she ran up the steps, calling out goodbyes to everyone.

At the top of the narrow lane two streets away Matthew was confronted by some children wearing cotton-wool Santa Claus beards and funny hats. One or two had hooked the beards onto dark glasses. In the dusk the small figures looked oddly unsettling, grotesque. They asked – politely enough – for a cigarette; Matthew was a non-smoker and told them so. Perhaps they took the explanation as a coded rebuke, but whatever the reason, they took offence. They moved in on him, knocking him to the ground, kicking, stamping. When Flora rounded the corner he was lifeless on the pavement, the attackers already out of sight.

She had always been so sensible, so positive – better than her sisters at helping Josie over the bad times, after her father died – that friends found it shocking how badly she took Matthew's death. She cried, it seemed, for weeks on end, her face distorted with despair; she made no attempt to maintain a stiff upper lip, nor to pull herself together. She was careless about bathing. She broke down in public and talked incessantly about Matthew, boring listeners into catalepsis. Her mother alone was excluded, her telephone messages and letters unanswered.

One day Josie turned up at the flat, and just went on knocking on the door until Flora let her in.

The flat was no longer immaculate. The lavishly decorated Christmas tree had shed its needles thickly onto the carpet; piled up around it, unopened, were the presents Flora and Matthew would have exchanged the day he died, the shiny giftwrap paper dulled with dust. Flora silently led the way into the kitchen where she began to open a tin of baked beans.

'I've called several times,' Josie said cautiously. 'I was beginning to worry –'

Flora broke in. 'I knew it would happen one day, of course,' she said. 'Him being so much older. I just didn't expect it so soon. One year.' She licked tomato sauce off her fingers, and wiped her fingers on her jeans. 'I suppose it was double that, really, because we were never apart. How many people do you know who spend all day and all night together? Going to the loo was the only time we had a closed door between us – and that was only because he was such a fucking prude. He said there were some things he preferred to do in private.' She wanted to say she had retorted, 'That's rich, considering the first time I set eyes on you, you were peeing in public,' but felt her mother might not appreciate the detail.

Josie filled the kettle and looked around for the tea. She glanced across at Flora, who had slid to the floor, knees drawn up, back against the fridge, and was eating the beans straight from the tin with a knife. She looked exhausted, but calm.

Flora said, 'Does this bother you?'

'What, the beans? No. I'm glad to see you're eating for a change.'

'That was Matthew. I sort of got into the habit. To please him. He worried.'

For a year, Josie wanted to say. He worried for just one year. What about all the years I spent worrying? But she stayed silent.

Flora said, 'I mean does this whole bit bother you. Me behaving badly.'

'You've had a dreadful shock —'

'So did you, when Dad died. But you didn't howl or anything. We never even talked about it once the funeral was over.'

Josie heard the anger and the accusation in the voice. She realised she was in the dock.

'I just didn't want the three of you to suffer more than you had to. I didn't want to load my loss onto you. Does that make sense?'

'Not a lot.'

Was this to be her punishment? To have Flora show her what grieving should be like? Flora, who knew nothing of nightly paroxysms, of racking groans stifled by pillows or covered up by late-night recitals on

Radio 3, who saw her emerge at breakfast with fashionably tinted glasses that disguised red, swollen eyes.

She said, flatly, 'It's hard to know what to do for the best. I wanted to protect you.'

'We never really dealt with the whole thing.'

Josie almost said, 'So you're dealing with it now,' but she swallowed the words just in time. Her throat ached and tears began to trickle down her cheeks.

Flora saw them, watched the tears for a moment, then she got up and put her arms round her mother and began to cry, easily, her face unravaged.

Josie held her tightly, her own painful tears falling onto Flora's sweater. Who was doing the comforting here, she wondered, who was being comforted?

The kettle began to whistle and Josie thought, thank God: we'll have a cup of tea and then we can begin to clean the flat. Sweep up the pine needles. Throw out that bloody tree.

In the rush of relief and maternal euphoria she spared a thought for Matthew, the innocent bystander, the necessary sacrifice. She felt a pang, but only momentarily: after all, she had hardly known him.

Tango
_____

Tango

There are many ways to chart the movement of the seasons: new walnuts, wet and slippery; Michaelmas, when rents are due and magistrates chosen; a blackberry swollen with inky juice sucked from the dark soil, all these signal the end of summer.

'There is a wind in a certain valley of the Andes,' he said, 'which carries the first hint of winter. Slides across your skin like iced taffeta.'

The transformation of Virginia creeper, crimson bleeding through the veins, seeping into the still-bright green, claiming it leaf by leaf, was the sign Gloria looked for. As the creeper flamed across the wire-netting fence of the used car showroom on the corner, and wool jackets in the new season's colour went into boutique windows, she had, as always, a sense of the equinox, a pause in the music of the spheres. This was the moment, the cusp of the year, with change in the air, when the subject of the office dance invariably came up. Could it be improved? Transformed in some way? Wild schemes – a DJ and light show, a Line Dance night, a warehouse rave – surfaced briefly. Died.

But now there came the new rep, a gaunt man, sallow-skinned, who had lived in Argentina, who spoke of skin and iced taffeta and talked eloquently of the tango when he and Gloria shared a table in the canteen one Friday. Geoffrey's grey cheeks bloomed, his eyes sparkled, as he described the sensual, dangerous rhythm of the dance, its complex social history – 'It began in the brothels on the waterfront, I'm sure you know that, Gloria. It was all pimps, whores and sailors, alcohol and knives, sex and death . . .' Her tea cooled while she listened.

On her way home she sidled into a record shop and bought a 'How to Tango' video. She pushed furniture to the walls and tried to learn, staring at the screen, at the parodic struttings and head-tossings of an irredeemably suburban pair in scarlet and black Lycra. She attempted to mimic their steps, rewound the tape, went doggedly through the paces. But without a partner, practice could go only so far.

When Geoffrey hesitated by her table a week or two later, tray poised before him, to ask if he could join her, she looked up at his face, framed against the cream gloss wall of the canteen and for a giddy moment experienced the magic of an invitation to the dance. From below, his chin was more prominent, his eyes glowed dark in their sockets. In the beat between question and answer she rose to her feet in one fluid movement, flung back her head and glided into his arms – or would have, but he had taken her acceptance for granted and plonked his tray down opposite hers.

As usual they talked of Argentina, but for Geoffrey it was not the colonial past, the struggle for independence, the disappointments of dictatorship that caught the imagination, it was the tango.

Gloria had been planning to take lessons of some sort anyway, it was what she did in the winter, to fill the empty evenings. When she was twenty she had enrolled for car maintenance at the local adult college. A magazine columnist declared it was the way to meet men: 'Sign on for French or History of Art and all you'll find are lonely women and pensioners. But get into car maintenance and you're there with the lads, muscles on view and good, honest sweat in the air.'

Whatever the columnist's experience and proclivities, car maintenance had presented difficulties, largely because Gloria had overlooked some basic practicalities: 'Students to provide handbook, jack and tool kit,' said the prospectus, adding encouragingly, 'explore the mechanical workings of your vehicle and cut motoring costs by servicing your own car.' Gloria felt it would be pointless to start buying jacks and tool kits; she did not own a car.

She had accepted that car maintenance was out. But

there was still navigation and seamanship – a male sort of area. Merely reading the description set her pulses racing: 'A course in astro-navigation and world-wide meteorology . . .' Adventure! The stars! The equinoctial quiver, a baring of the wintry fangs. Why not?

She began to fill in the form. The small print added, 'A knowledge of terrestrial navigation and basic meteorology is assumed.'

She signed on for nineteenth-century narratives. She had always liked *Middlemarch* – would that be a nineteenth-century narrative? She hoped so. Dorothea, who put up with life's disappointments and made the best of things was, she felt, the sort of heroine she understood.

There were the usual women of a certain age, and the usual sprightly pensioners, but there was a quiet man who shared his copy of Gissing's *Born in Exile* and bought her a coffee in the break.

The teacher had seemed quite old to Gloria, though, fifteen years later, she realised the woman could have been no more than thirty-five, the age Gloria was now. She singled out the young pair for special attention and told them one day that she herself had been born in exile of a sort in some outpost of what had once been Empire. Miss Ross had grown animated, talking of distant horizons and the lure of the far-away. They stuck the class for a term, and felt traitorous, abandoning her, but after a while it seemed pointless to slog off to the adult college in order to sit side by side when his or her bedsit was so much more comfortable. It lasted for two years and ended only when his firm posted her lover to Liverpool. She could have followed him; perhaps she should have made that clearer. There was a day when she came close to spelling it out; another when she felt certain he was working up to a declaration, but there was a failure of nerve somewhere. On his part? On hers? The words did not get said. The crucial moment passed and it was 'I'll miss you dreadfully' instead of 'I can't live without you.' Parting was not death, of course. People survive. So, now, listening to tales of the Argentine, she signed up for tango lessons.

Mr Fuentes was short and plump and courtly. He instructed her in the *paseo*, the open turn, the Valentino. She persevered, and began to master the movements: the knife-blade sharpness of the swivel, the controlled swoop. Before long she was wearing her hair smoothed back in a Latin manner, had abandoned comfort in favour of high-heeled shoes and slinky skirts – especially on Fridays.

After one session when Mr Fuentes had taught her – in a most respectable way possible – the correct manner of sliding her instep up the back of his fat little leg, a gesture that Gloria accomplished though feeling somewhat ridiculous, it came to her that there was a way she could fulfil her teacher's exhortations to 'Practise, Miss McKenzie, you must practise,' and at the same time open Geoffrey's eyes to her terpsichorean skill.

Back at the office she raised the matter of the firm's dance: surely it was up to them all to move with the times? She threw out a lure to the younger girls: they had been through their Gipsy Kings phase, and the salsa, fast and furious. The older ones remembered the heyday of the cha-cha and the samba. Why not make this year Latin America Night? Suggestion slips were duly filled in. Not often did the Social Committee Minutes record the phrase 'Carried Unanimously', but they did at the next meeting.

Gloria realised that she would probably have to sit out those dances Mr Fuentes had not prepared her for, but that was a detail: the tango was the thing, the pinnacle. Together she and Geoffrey would twirl and stamp, they would glitter like stars in the firmament.

She waited impatiently for Friday, when Geoffrey would be in, setting up appointments and doing his expenses. But when, at lunch, she gave him the news about the dance he let fall casually that his wife would be coming up from Leatherhead for the occasion. Gloria put down her fork, the chicken-and-mushroom pie turned to dead-sea fruit. The Wife. Pliant and hip-swivelling, the Wife would be in his arms at the dance.

'That's nice,' she said.

She scoured her meagre address book and came up with a man met long ago at an Internet workshop, who might serve as camouflage at least. She e-mailed him an invitation, using the office equipment, a clear breach of the rules. He was otherwise engaged.

At the next lesson her feet were leaden, her movements clumsy. Mr Fuentes was puzzled.

'Miss McKenzie, are you unwell? Where is the fire? The spirit?'

The rehearsal room was lined with mirrors; on one wall a radiator bulked like a set of organ pipes, clanking unmusically from time to time. She looked at their reflections, a pale, thin woman in a blouse and skirt, and Mr Fuentes, whose head reached her chin; sixtyish, portly, in his baggy trousers and cracked patent pumps. They made an improbable couple, but not an impossible one. He had dignity. And in motion, he was impressive.

'Mr Fuentes,' she said, 'how'd you like to earn some extra cash?'

He was reluctant at first; a triple session was not to be sneezed at, but his evenings were busy enough with normal lessons, and Mrs Fuentes expected him for family dinner. In the end it was not the pathos of Gloria's predicament that convinced him but her fierceness. 'It's for the tango,' she said. He capitulated.

On the day of the dance, Gloria left the office early and had her hair coiled sleekly, with a flat curl stuck to one cheek. She put on her new black dress and took a taxi to the hall. Fearful that Mr Fuentes might be disconcerted by the crowd, she arrived early. At first the foyer was deserted, then more people began to arrive, streaming past her, the girls shedding woollen coats, emerging like butterflies in scarlet, emerald and blue. Those she knew, she waved at cheerfully and called out that she was waiting for her partner – 'See you inside!' From the ballroom she heard the musicians strike up, the sound of voices, laughter. Shivering in the draught from the swing doors, she paced the foyer, watching latecomers hurry in. She was at the far end of the lobby when the receptionist called her name.

'Someone here for you.'

Standing at the desk was a young boy – twenty-something – looking irritable. Gloria hurried over and drew him away from the receptionist's inquisitive eye and cocked ear.

'You wanted me?'

'Dad's been taken ill. He didn't want you to be stood wondering where he was. He said to tell you he's sorry.' His voice was mechanical.

Tango

From within there came a burst of applause as a cha-cha came to an end, then a buzz of chatter. Gloria stared at the messenger of doom. She felt numb. She had seen Geoffrey sauntering in, earlier, at his side a colourless woman with stiffly set hair and bad legs. But the colourless woman had an identity: she was one half of a couple. Gloria could not brave the ballroom alone; she would simply collect her coat and leave. She would tell them tomorrow that she had been taken ill. Flu, she would explain, or food poisoning. Suspected E-coli. Any excuse would do. She saw that the boy was impatient to be off, glancing out to the street.

'Thank you,' she said. To her dismay, her eyes filled with tears.

He frowned. 'Look,' he said, 'if it's a partner you're short of, I could stand in for my dad, for a bit.'

She studied him briefly: the collarless white shirt, dark jeans and jacket might pass in the crowd. Black hair scraped into a pony-tail, olive-skin, lustrous almond eyes. He was, she realised, beautiful. And, best of all, he was taller than she was. But how was he to be explained?

'Could you pretend to be Spanish?' Gloria asked.

'Leave it out,' he said impatiently. 'I *am* Spanish.' The London accent contrasted disconcertingly with his brooding Mediterranean looks. A conversation could only lead to disaster; she would be revealed for what she

was, a pathetic creature who had bought herself a professional partner.

'I mean could you pretend not to understand English?'

He shrugged. 'Whatever.'

Together they entered the ballroom. Gloria had deliberately waited until she heard the strains of a tango, so
that they could go straight out onto the floor. She placed
herself in the circle of his arms, back arched, head up.
He felt her shaking and pulled her close, authoritative.

'Relax, wait for the music. Drag, don't rush. Never
hurry, OK . . .'

She had followed Mr Fuentes obediently, diligently
copied his steps. Now, for the first time, she experienced
the dizzy reality. Fused from hip to shoulder they moved
as one. He bent his head, his lips brushing her ear, murmuring precise instructions.

Everyone was aware of them, the tall, angular young
man and the woman in the black swirly dress with the
spiky, sexy, high-heeled shoes, gliding languorously,
pausing with the beat of an indrawn breath, then on,
fleet flashing like scissors. The girls from Gloria's office
exchanged glances, eyebrows raised. Impressed.
Surprised. A toy-boy, a kiss-curl and a split skirt. Gloria,
of all people! She, magnificent, haughty as an empress,
ignored them all.

Between dances, she faced the ordeal of chatting to

people she knew, but she kept the introductions firmly minimal. 'This is Roberto, he doesn't speak English and I must get us something to drink.' And she hurried him away.

At one point, as they were pausing on the edge of the floor, Geoffrey appeared at her elbow, a glass of wine in each hand.

'Gloria. I had no idea . . . You must save me a dance. I'll just get rid of these.' He moved away.

She turned to Roberto urgently.

'I must leave. I can't –'

'Rubbish. You'll be fine. Take it easy. Walk it.'

When Geoffrey took her onto the floor she went rigid with nerves, mouth dry, armpits wet. Then she caught Roberto's eye, the little downward movement of his hand that said: don't rush, and she allowed herself to be led into the dance.

Geoffrey was fulsome with compliments, she saw him looking at her in a different way as he took her back to Roberto. He began to say, 'We must do this again some time –' but she turned away before he had altogether finished. Geoffrey was just another grey man. He held no mystery.

The music was about to start again, but Roberto was glancing surreptitiously at his watch. 'How long does this caper go on, then?'

Guilty, she said, 'Are you bored? Of course, you must
be –'

'It's not that. But I don't want to miss the last train. I
have to get back to Chingford.'

Chingford. The spin and drag of the Buenos Aires
waterfront swirled in her head, the coloured lights flit-
tered across the room like liquid jewels; she felt the heat
of the sun, the fire in the blood and because of the
pathetic scheduling of British Rail or whatever it was
called these days, the golden coach was about to revert
to pumpkin: the boy had to get back to Chingford.

'Look,' she said, 'I'll pay for a cab, how's that?'

He hesitated, then shrugged acceptance, and took up
his position, pulling her close, the hollow of his cheek
fitting her sleek head. Her body sagged against his, and
thigh to thigh, they moved off smoothly, and now, eyes
closed, she needed no instruction. The music filled her
head. He guided her, but she knew where the true
authority lay: Dorothea was redundant here. Tonight
she was Lola Montez, Carmen, Evita. While the music
played.

A Sense of Isolation

A Sense of Isolation

Henderson got off the train and walked towards the harbour, carrying his belongings in a blue canvas zipper bag. He asked no one for directions, and carried no map, but threaded his way instinctively through the network of the streets that led towards the sea.

It was a small town and he quickly passed through the residential area to the shopping mall, the hotels and the park that overlooked the bay. He walked on, to the bulky retaining wall and the narrow beach beyond it, his shoes crunching on the shingle. When he could go no further, when he reached the line where land became water, he dropped the bag and sat down, drawing his feet in towards him. The insistent surf licked the shore six inches from his toes. The Indian Ocean filled his line of vision.

He stayed on the beach until the sun sank low, shining into his eyes, blinding him. He considered moving on: he could climb aboard the next train and disappear. His presence here would go unremarked; he would have formed no bond to be broken; there would be no gap where he once filled a place. He and the town, unchanged, would occupy their different spaces; remoteness, after all, was a matter of condition as well as location. His isolation would simply be transferred from one setting to another. Pull out, then? Wasn't that the pattern? Further down the beach a child ran on ahead of his mother, then paused, lifting and lowering his feet into the shallow surf with care, like a long-legged bird looking for food. He flung back his head and the sound of laughter drifted back along the shore.

Henderson got up, stiffly, and retraced his steps, past the hotels and the shopping mall and stopped at the entrance of a low, pink-painted house whose window offered Bed and Breakfast. He rang the bell.

After a day or two everyone knew that Mrs Menzies – Sal to them all – had a new lodger, an Englishman, quiet, fortyish, pale, plump, with a receding hairline, who while not on holiday was not, apparently, in town on business either. He seemed at a loose end.

The woman in the health food store greeted him on his second visit and asked in the straightforward Aussie way if he was planning to stay long. Henderson seemed unsure.

'For a while,' he said. 'Maybe for longer.'

'If you're staying, you could come along to one of our groups,' she suggested, 'we've got an art circle and a drama group, and we do poetry readings –'

'I'm not much of a joiner,' he said. 'Thanks anyway.'

Each day he was down at the harbour, and later by the strand, watching the children fishing or clambering about on the rocks. If one of the children asked him a question, there would be an exchange or two, until Henderson moved on, abruptly, as though recalling an appointment.

Mrs Menzies attempted to engage him in conversation for the first day or so, and then gave up. A widow, she too found silence a natural condition. But one morning, when she brought in his breakfast, she found him looking at a book, a history of Australia, plucked from the shelf in the front room.

'You can borrow it if you like. You'll learn a lot from that book.'

'I've read it.'

'Oh yes?'

'Yes.' There was a pause.

'Well then,' she said.

He added, as though to explain a lack of opinion, 'It was a long time ago.' He put the book back on the shelf and turned to his breakfast.

Years before, fresh from university, he had enrolled for evening classes in car maintenance, with the doomed ambition of springing this unsuspected practical skill on his surprised father. Most of the class were lonely people, there in search of friendship or something even less likely, and in the coffee-break he met a dark-haired girl who was studying the nineteenth-century novel. She had a breathless enthusiasm that caught his interest and without thought or guilt he abandoned the combustion engine, borrowed his mother's copy of Gissing's *Born in Exile* and embraced literature and, in due course, the dark-haired girl. Miss Ross, the teacher, had talked to them once, over coffee, about her childhood in some far-away place, India perhaps, her placid face suddenly vivid as she spoke of the uninterrupted vastness of skies that reduced the human to an ant. Distant places, unknown to her listeners, she conjured up one by one, and as she uttered the names they sprang to life like stars winking into view at nightfall: the Himalayas, the Gobi – the great Mongolian desert the Chinese call the sea of sand – and Patagonia, with its wind that cuts like a knife. The sense of distance could create a problem, she said, 'It can affect the soul.' She laughed, to take the curse off the phrase. And then she talked of the sense of isolation experienced by Australians on the western seaboard, how it had created a collective neurosis. 'They have a smaller population per square mile than almost anywhere else on earth. There are cattle stations in the Kimberley the size of Scotland.' The coffee break ended before Henderson could learn more, but she lent him a book, the one now on Mrs Menzies' shelf. Quite soon after that he abandoned the class and had failed to return the book.

Market research proved a convenient career: he travelled, organised anything from a seminar to a group soup-tasting. Professionally impersonal, as the job required, he kept his distance. And in search, perhaps, of an unfound anchorage, Henderson learned to love the trains that carried him from city to city. On the train there was always hope of change. Now and then, encouraged by a tangled glance, an encounter that seemed to encourage optimism, he embarked on the precarious negotiations of a relationship. There was a girl or two, a bed or two, but in the end, a dying fall, something to do with failure of nerve, perhaps.

Promotion brought an end to the travelling; others organised; he analysed, weighed up, advised. As he grew older, the solitary condition began to exact its own imperatives; like a nautilus mollusc he constructed his own shell around him, outgrowing one solitary chamber only to build himself a bigger and better replacement. And with the passing of time he gained increasing first-hand experience of a sense of isolation, though in his case the landscapes were interior ones, the featureless reaches of the mind, the distances black as space.

He made half-hearted efforts, earlier on, replied to a few personal ads, but the offers of 'Friendship, leading to' led nowhere, the women instinctively drawing back from the gravitational pull of his despair.

They tried: 'Make me laugh,' one of them invited. And another: 'Tell me about yourself.'

He shook his head. 'Usual boring biography.'

'There's no such thing,' she retorted, frustrated. 'In its own way each life is an epic.'

'An epic can also be boring,' he said, and raised the matter of dinner: there was a new Chinese place they might try.

He attempted an ad for himself once; why not? He sat, poised over his laptop, the cursor blinking balefully, and no words came. He tapped out HELP HELP HELP, and drew a bottle round the words, but there was no one to send the message to.

'You're so . . . impervious,' one of the women told him. 'I'd like to stick a pin into you, see what happens.' He was tempted to encourage her: Try, why don't you? But he let it pass.

He thought of himself as one of the hollow men, stuffed with straw. If you pricked him, would he bleed? Not noticeably. Just as pain cannot be registered on an X-ray, suffering is not always defined by visibility. An old movie poster he noticed one day had it that in space no one can hear you scream. Nor closer to home, if you learn the art of screaming silently.

Whisky and pills were helpful, and he learned to use the whisky with discretion: he drank steadily, without becoming an embarrassment. Glassy-eyed, he might hesitate at the wine merchant's check-out, but he never got falling-down drunk or dribbled on his clothes. He held onto his job. Still, there were times when the pressure became hard to bear. On one of these he picked up the phone and asked the operator to test his line.

'I'll call you back,' she said. He sat, letting the phone ring on, so that the room was filled with this sound that shrank the space between people. ('Where are you calling from, operator?' he wanted to ask. 'How far away are you? What distance are we talking about?') That was the day he tossed up between extreme alternatives and took a plane to Australia. Not straight to Perth, that would have been premature: his first landfall should be Sydney, as it had been for those first outsiders, a flotilla freighted not only by human cargo but the chains worn by the unwilling passengers. He would make his way slowly to the place that had for so long flickered at the back of his thoughts. He would take the train from coast to coast, from Sydney to Perth.

He walked his way through Sydney to the rail station, and at 14.55 the Indian Pacific pulled out. Three nights

on the train, nearly three thousand miles to cover. He
would inch his way across the continent, crawling,
beetle-like, eating the miles as the track bore him west-
wards. The first morning, as the rising sun was left
behind, the silvery light had a clarity that etched detail
into rocks and vegetation. At noon the sun sat overhead
and the landscape shimmered its emptiness at him. But at
evening the low, slanting beams, lengthening the train
by its own shadow, glittered against the dusty glass of
the windows, lent mystery to passing shapes and turned
the rusty track to flame. He had a sleeper – a room to
himself – and lay, hour after hour on his berth, steadily
getting through the bottles he carried in his canvas bag,
staring out at the moving sky and the bare earth, the
monotony broken by the pale, ghostly bark of an occasional gum tree. He disappointed gregarious fellow-
travellers by failing to enter into the spirit of the journey
and exchange life stories. When the train called at
Adelaide he stayed in his compartment: big cosmopoli-
tan cities were not on his map. He looked out for the
romantic place-names he had read about – Port Augusta,
Tarcoola, Broken Hill, Kalgoorlie – stages on an old
adventure, when camels plodded the course the steel
ladders would follow across the Nullarbor Plain.

At dinner on the second night his solitary table was
invaded by two small children, who spilled the salt and

giggled shyly at him from behind the menu, which they proceeded to read aloud. He encouraged them, and reassured their parents.

'The kids bothering you, mate?'

'Not at all. They're advising me what to order.'

He remembered mealtimes with his own parents, two professionals seated across the table from one another, eating quickly, without much interest in the food. Between mouthfuls they talked about work, the conversational ball bouncing fast. From the sideline, the child listened, admiring, an onlooker outside their game.

'Shall we go for a walk?' he might ask, but they were busy, talking, listening to each other and the question went unanswered.

He planned for years how to impress them: come first in class. Get a gold star. Win a prize. Anything to break in, cause them to pause in mid-discussion and turn his way. He was untalented at sport and had small hopes of the school play: he was too often cast as a spear carrier or 'crowd' to warrant parental pride. Until, in a much-curtailed version of *The Wind in the Willows*, he was Mr Toad. Not many lines, but much flamboyant leaping about and loud exclamations of 'Poop-poop!'

Rehearsals went well. He zigzagged the stage in a cardboard cut-out motor car and showed off with bravado. On the night, he donned a padded vest to provide bulk, and buttoned himself into the loud checked suit. Goggles, driving gloves and he was ready. But as the hall filled, he noted that the seats assigned to his parents were empty. It was unlike them to be late. Anxiously he peered through a chink in the curtain, closed his eyes and counted to fifty, peeped again. When the warning bell sounded he faced the fact that they were going to miss the play. The audience enjoyed *The Wind in the Willows* but nobody enthused about Mr Toad.

The train arrived in Perth, early in the morning, on a day which was autumn to Henderson but here they called it spring, and he breathed air that smelled like the Mediterranean, that held the scent of flowers with a hint of the sea, and promise of more warmth to come. This place, the teacher of nineteenth-century narratives had told him so long ago, was further away from the nearest city than anywhere else on earth. How could that be? What could that mean? Isolation, for sure. In his mind he had held a picture of distance and of silence. But Perth seethed. It was a city of concrete canyons: tall, white and modern. What had once been the Swan River settlement rose from the water, the sharpness of steel and glass catching the sun. Traffic and people, noise and movement surrounded him. Buffeted, Henderson took refuge, as always, on a train. He got off at a pink and blue painted town with not a high-rise in sight, and he walked down to the harbour and gazed out at the sea.

Ahead of him lay what people called emptiness, but of course what they meant was distance. Distance between one place and another, between one person and another. Not emptiness but isolation. The condition of detachment. This sea was six thousand miles wide. At its most profound, two thousand miles deep. If he were to slip into the dark waters and just keep going, he would come in time to the dagger point of South America – to Patagonia, Tierra del Fuego, the land of fire. And of wind. Birds flew those distances, fragile wings beating through the skies, their hollow-boned bodies resting lightly on the back of the wind. A man was tied to the earth.

At night the harbour became *Alice in Wonderland* territory, nature reversed, the moon inverted, huge and golden, Orion sunk low, the Southern Cross blazing. In this reversal he found a kind of comfort, isolation approached intimacy. The light from the stars was so bright that he tilted his cap over his eyes as though shielding himself from sunlight. By day, walking for miles along the beach, recording the changes in the light, the unfurling of leaves, the patterns in a rock formation, he sometimes stopped to watch the children, boys playing ball, a schoolgirl practising ballet steps, light as a sea-bird, her footprints barely visible in the hard, wet sand. One day she spoke to him – 'What are you staring at?' – and he told her he was watching the way her shadow danced with her, like a partner.

She nodded, raising and lowering her arm, watching her shadow wave back.

'My mum was wondering what you do. Back home?'

He tried to think of an acceptable way to explain market research to the child.

'I find out what people think they want so that someone can give it to them.'

'Sort of Santa Claus,' she said.

He laughed and moved off, turning his back on the sun and the sea.

'If you like dancing,' she called after him, 'we're putting on a show, at school. Saturday week. You could come.'

The first time he called in for his snapshots the man in the shop handed him the folder and commented, 'Been taking shots of the cliffs, eh? They're bare now but wait till we get a bit of rain, there'll be purple mulla-mulla flowers all over the place.'

Henderson would not normally have entered into conversation, but then 'normally', at home, he would have been handed his developed prints without comment.

'I wanted them bare. To show the cliff formation –'

'Right on. Funny stuff, spongelite. All those marine sponges, dead animals lying on the sea floor for thirty million years. And now they're cliffs. Makes you think.' He handed Henderson his change. 'Have a good day.'

The woman in the health food shop wrapped his sandwich of Italian cheese and local salad. 'You're still here, then.'

Out walking one day he rounded the headland at the far end of the bay and came upon a group of people seated in a circle, listening to one of their number reading aloud. The flat, Australian vowels and no-nonsense delivery gave a conversational tone to the lines that drifted across the sand to where he stood:

'Since once I sat upon a promontory,
And heard a mermaid on a dolphin's back
Uttering such dulcet and harmonious breath,
That the rude sea grew civil at her song,
And certain stars shot madly from their spheres
To hear the sea-maid's music –'

Someone called out, 'Did you see that whale last week, over the other side of the bluff?' The woman from the health stores waved to Henderson. He waved back and moved on as the reading continued. Midsummer dreaming in spring, which was really autumn, seemed oddly right in this isolated, perhaps enchanted, landscape.

The following Saturday he set off for the harbour, carrying his blue canvas bag, restocked at the local bottle shop. He never intended to see the school dancing display, but later, watching the seagulls skimming the waves and landing with precision on their chosen patch of sand, he changed his mind. He walked back to town, and past the shopping mall, where his landlady, carrying a newspaper, waved to him and called out where was he going in such a hurry? Country music was spilling from the hi-fi shop next door and she had to shout above the noise. Momentarily elated by the warmth of the sun on his bald patch, Henderson waved his bag and called a reply: '. . . the kids . . . a few shots.'

Mrs Menzies watched him go, and waited at the kerb for the lights to change. She glanced at the front page and stood, traffic forgotten, to read the headlined story. Then she began to hurry along the pavement, breaking into a clumsy run.

There were signposts to the dancing display, to be held in 'the hall', a one-storey shack ringed with flowering bushes. Henderson waited for a while, pacing up and down the garden, until he heard the music, then went in.

Plastic chairs were ranged in rows between him and

the little stage. He faced a sea of parental backs in bright summer dresses or shirts. On-stage, girls in gauzy white skirts clustered self-consciously. He saw the bird-like child from the beach, in line with the others, hands linked in a chain, her long neck extended, attempting the transformation from gull into swan.

Henderson was aware of a lowering of spirits; a desolation that sucked the energy from his limbs and threatened to immobilise him where he stood. He was having trouble breathing, and hugged the blue bag to his chest, the roaring in his head crackling like static. The smell of the place, the stage, the counterpoint of children and parents, reawakened a woe, a terror closed off and forgotten.

'Poop-poop!' went Mr Toad, and the curtains drew together jerkily as the parents applauded. Cast and audience mingled cheerfully, but for Mr Toad there was an urgent message: someone coming to collect him; a problem at home.

A stroke. A stroke was something you gave a cat, the fur warm under your fingers. His mother always told him to stroke the piano keys, gently, when he played. A stroke couldn't be very bad, then.

He sat by the hospital bed dry-eyed while his father held her white hand and wept. 'Let me in!' he shouted silently, seeing them wrapped, as always, in each other.

His lungs were bursting, deprived of air, as though a glass bell had closed over him.

He forced himself, now, to breathe, to move forward with the exaggerated, half-crouching gait of the late arrival, towards the row of seats nearest the door, but paused, put down his bag and reached into it, feeling for his camera. Through the music he was vaguely aware of noise from the doorway, the sound of people, and half-turned, still fumbling in the bag, when he was knocked to the ground, his arms twisted behind him, while screams and cries of alarm filled the air, drowning out the taped Tchaikovsky.

The performance was cancelled. With half the girls in tears and a member of the audience briefly under arrest, the sparkle had gone from cygnets and swans alike.

Later there were apologies, attempts at explanation –

'What can I say?' Mrs Menzies' voice was wobbly, her face crumpled. 'I saw the stuff in the paper and . . . Look, I'm really sorry.'

She stood now, the paper in her hands, the newsprint creased into illegibility. She blamed herself for the whole thing.

Henderson himself was only too keen to bring the incident to a close.

'Please don't give it a thought, these things happen.'

They happen to Mr Toad.

'No problem,' he said, adopting their argot.

Relieved parents reacted with determined good humour: silly business, but no harm done, eh? They were excessively friendly, now that trust had gone.

At moonrise he was on the beach, the blue bag by his side. He sat for a long time, watching the slow movement of the waves, barely visible in the darkness as he finished the bottle.

He thought about that other man, the loner who had carried a gun, not a bottle, in his bag. Did he flourish the gun, spinning, spraying the schoolroom with bullets, seeing the bodies flail and fall, saving the final burst for himself, falling among them, exploding in an ecstasy of belonging? Henderson tried to imagine the moment. Was that how it had been? With the lethargy of a deep exhaustion he began to scoop up handfuls of sand, slowly at first, then picking up a rhythm. He scooped the sand with his fingers, the tips sore, almost raw, as the bag filled.

When he felt it was heavy enough, he shoved in the empty bottle, zipped the bag shut and adjusted the carrying strap for shoulder length. Then he stood up, staggering slightly, lifted it over his head and settled the bag at his side. He walked slowly into the dark water, noticing how the light of the moon lay on the blue-black water like a ribbon of gauze. Could a dolphin ride that wavering road, carrying a mermaid? He felt a sudden ache of sorrow in his chest, so sharp that he almost cried aloud, but as always, he was silent. He wondered how long he would be able to keep to the shimmering path as he headed out into the distance.

*

On the terrace of the National Theatre overlooking the Thames, waiting for the matinee to begin, a retired teacher of English literature sipped her wine and leafed through the paper. On the Foreign News pages a brief story about an unfortunate incident in Western Australia caught her eye – 'Briton Dies in Drowning Accident. Tragic end to holiday.' In her younger days Susan would have read it with interest, but Australia no longer engaged her. On the next page she saw a headline about the restoration of a Piero della Francesca fresco, and folded back the paper to read the report more comfortably.

Reading Lessons

Reading Lessons

'I'll teach you to read,' he said.

Most people don't remember learning to read. Ask them and they'll come up with the first book they enjoyed, or they'll vaguely recall a sense of mother, lap, armchair. Or a classroom filled with the noise of other children. I remember.

He taught me quietly, carefully, building up the vocabulary I would be needing. I would be using.

'Hand,' he said. 'See the word: HAND. This is my hand. Touch it.'

It began like that, with body parts.

He wrote out the words on squares of white card, in capital letters, using a thick, black, felt-tipped pen.

'Legs,' he said. 'Look at the word: LEGS. Learn the word.'

In the summer, we had the lessons in the garden, and he taught me CAT and MOUSE, HIDE and SEEK, using the cards. Neighbours would see us, over the fence, see the good father, reading lessons in progress. They made remarks to my mother when we met in the street and smiled at me, the good child, learning to read so young.

We always had the lessons in the same place, sprawled out on the grass, the earth beneath our bodies warm from the sun, moist. In time, the grass where we lay grew pale, flattened. Deprived of light, it looked sickly.

He held up the cards and we practised. My mother went in and out of the house, banging doors, pulling out weeds or clipping at things, taking no part, telling him to leave the child alone, let her have a bit of peace, but the lessons went on.

'Mouth,' he said. 'See the word: MOUTH. Touch my mouth.'

There were other words, and I learned them too. First came description, then instruction: OPEN. HOLD. STROKE. FAST. HARD.

Afterwards I found out these were verbs, adverbs, adjectives, but I learned them as orders to be obeyed.

When it grew colder and the grass chilled my bare legs, we continued the lessons indoors, my mother busy clattering pans in the kitchen. There were new, simple words: TABLE. Touch the table. BOOK. Open the book.

Later, when he came to my room, the practical lessons took place. Nothing spoken now, just the written words, thick black letters on white cards, held up for me to see: OPEN. HOLD. STROKE. HARD. HARDER.

Now there were new words, difficult to understand, to

explain, but they too had to be learned. First the words, then the actions.

The teachers, when I began school, were puzzled. The child knew how to read, she had been well taught, she had a good vocabulary, no problems there. Why, then, they asked, did she cry, silently, unstoppably, when the reading lessons began?

They asked me, but explanations were impossible. What words would I have used? Screaming was useful: when I began screaming they stopped asking questions.

A man came round once to talk to us. To me. Just a few questions, he said, nothing to be afraid of, but of course there was. By then the cards had shown me the words for silence, for secret and for punishment.

My vocabulary grew; there were words I taught myself, though not written down: words like knives. Words like hate. Then escape. As always, first came the words, then the action.

Most days, now, I like to sit here, in the same place. In summer the ground beneath me is warmed by the sun. In winter it is less agreeable, but I like the familiarity, the feeling of the solid wall at my back. And I use the cards, as he did then. I hold them up for others to read. HOME-LESS, one says. And HUNGRY. And PLEASE HELP.

Internal Injuries

Internal Injuries

She swings off the road and brings them deftly into the car park. In the dull glow of an overhead lamp she can just make out the directions on a sign-board: Left for Reception. Right for General Wards and – some graffiti artist has been at work here – Straight on for eternity. The tarmac has a greasy sheen, the bushes planted round the squat building look lifeless, metallic in the harsh sodium glare of the lamp-post.

Two ambulance men are busy unloading a stretcher, another throws blankets into a large basket and wheels it away rapidly, avoiding eye-contact.

She manages to get him out of the car, but he is heavy, leaning on her, limping as she helps him across the parking lot to the scuffed, wooden swing doors and over to the Reception desk. The woman on night duty looks tired; she waits, the muscles of her face slack, for one of them to speak.

'My husband –' Bridget begins, but he cuts in.

'Fell down the stairs. May have broken . . .' he hesitates, unsure which bone to choose.

'I'll give you a number. The Sister will assess you.'

Bridget helps him over to the row of plastic chairs and he lowers himself, wincing.

She glances across at a drinks dispensing machine. 'Fancy a Coke?'

'Better not. Only make me want to pee.'

The strip lighting casts a shadowless, unflattering glare on the room and the people in it: a middle-aged pair two seats away; a young couple, cradling a child between them; two girls in their twenties; two men clutching motorcycle helmets as though for comfort; a teenage boy in a leather jacket, slumped alone, cursing quietly to himself. From beyond another pair of swing doors, pierced by glass portholes, she can hear voices; a child crying, a man calling out, repeating the same phrase – 'Will somebody help me?' – footsteps, some hurried, some measured. Telephones ringing.

'I suppose we'll be stuck here for hours,' Dan is predicting, when a nurse appears, levers him into a wheelchair and pushes him away briskly like a shopper heading for the supermarket check-out. They vanish into a cubicle at the far end of the room.

Bridget glances around at the chipped paintwork, the worn green floor-covering, the rows of red plastic seats, some with yellowish foam creaming like pus from jagged rips in the grimy leatherette covering. What kind of person, she wonders, would attack the seats while waiting in Casualty? She blinks, rubbing her hand across her eyes as if to wipe off dust. It is only nine-thirty.

The elderly woman nearby gives her an encouraging, motherly smile.

'He'll be all right.'

'Of course he will. At worst it's only a fracture, and it probably isn't even that.'

The woman looks shocked, her smile redundant, somehow no longer appropriate. Bridget can read her thoughts: what kind of person would speak so unfeelingly about her injured husband? Bridget could tell her: the kind of person who not more than an hour ago had been yelling at him to bugger off and take his gear with him. He had slammed out of the flat and was on his way to the front door when he tripped on a bit of worn lino and went headlong down the stairs –

– and if he'd been more careful, he'd probably be sharing a takeaway with a mate by now, and I'd be watching the News, not sitting in Casualty picking at plastic foam.

The nurse has finished her assessment. She resettles Dan in his seat. 'You'll be called when the doctor's free. Watch the sign.' She nods at the wall. The electronic panel pulses with red dots forming a number. Discouraging messages flash on and off: CURRENT ESTIMATED WAITING TIME: ONE HOUR THIRTY MINUTES.

The young couple sit silent, the child inert in their

arms. The sound of crying suddenly intensifies from the mysterious territory beyond the swing doors, then dies away. In this place there's no laughter in the next room. The youth in the leather jacket gets to his feet and begins wandering unsteadily about, chewing at his lips, blood dripping steadily from the ragged dressing on his hand. The two young girls – Americans, Bridget now realises – are reading aloud to each other from the tattered magazines scattered around them.

'Listen to this!' one cries softly, and reads out a horoscope predicting fame, fortune and the imminence of a tall dark stranger. They smile, showing perfect teeth, and laugh together, wrapped in an intimacy in no way impinged on by the stares they attract. They continue to check the horoscope page. 'It's a year old,' one of them comments cheerfully, 'but, hey, that's OK.' Both girls have long, lustrous hair, glowing skin, big eyes, generous breasts; they touch a lot, and examine each other's make-up and nail polish with care. One slowly brushes tangles from the other's hair and pins it up, absorbed in the detail of the physical task. They sprawl on the plastic seats, graceful as cats, their movements fluid, relaxed. The dark-haired girl has one foot bare, she leans forward, looking at the toes.

'I think it's septic. It's definitely septic. What will they do?'

The boy in the leather jacket has lurched into the assessment cubicle, demanding attention. He begins to unwind his bandage, and bigger splodges of blood drip, dark on the green lino. The Sister calls another nurse and they chide him, without rancour. 'Oh Kevin, you're such a bad boy. Look what you've done now . . .' They redo his bandage, tell him to get himself a Coke from the machine, the doctor won't be long. He lopes over, puts in a coin, pulls the handle and waits, studying the machine hopefully, like a gambler waiting for the jackpot. Nothing. He kicks it, moodily, without anger, and reaches down as the can clatters into view. The windows are sealed. The room is airless, and a low hum from some ventilation plant vibrates unsettlingly in Bridget's head –

– *this is just an ante-room; judgements are made elsewhere, through the swing doors with the port-holes. And can I ask for assessment too? Tell me what's wrong . . .*

From the street, cutting through the smog of traffic noise, a jazz trumpet weaves a brassy filigree, faint but pure, then fades, like sky-writing blurring into space. A bang, a crash; drama as doors fly open and a man in a wheelchair, oxygen mask clamped to his face, is brought in at the run by an ambulance attendant.

'Up the para-Olympics!' Kevin calls, waving his Coke.

A woman, fortyish, plump body encased in a tight
pink frock, trots on high heels, trying to keep up with the
wheelchair. Her hair is a surprisingly bright yellow and
there are gold rings on her fleshy fingers. The wheelchair vanishes through the swing doors and they bang
shut, leaving her behind. She provides Reception
with the necessary details. Bridget catches odd words:
'. . . collapsed without warning . . . having a few
drinks –' The woman looks round the waiting room,
trying to catch someone's eye.

'Mustn't grumble, I suppose. In sickness and in health,
eh?' She laughs and without warning begins to cry noisily. The middle-aged couple look away, embarrassed.

– in sickness and in health, right. To have and to hold,
from this day forward, for better for worse . . . to love and to
cherish . . . and the next bit, the dangerous bit that brings on a
pain like an ice-cream ache behind the eyes, the threat of tears
that will disarm you, rob you of strength, leave you remem-
bering how it felt that day, almost a year ago – with this ring
I thee wed, with my body I thee worship . . . With my body I
thee worship, and here comes the ache, the tears, but they must
be fought off. Blink hard, fast, that's the way –

She is aware of Dan beside her, clearing his throat,
wincing as he moves.

– it's a well-known fact: marriage is not easy . . . major
surgery is easy: lie back and let them get on with it.

Marriage is difficult. Minefields to be got through, power bases to be held or abandoned, sensitivities to be skirted . . . it's not what you expect. The demands, no space of your own, an unnatural condition –

The American girls rest quietly together, feeding one another mouthfuls of a chocolate bar. The two men with helmets are questioned by the yellow-haired woman:

'Did you have an accident?'

'It's our mate. He's in there.' In the next room. Or maybe he's been moved, to radiography, the operating theatre, intensive care . . . through the swing doors lie territories Bridget doesn't want to think about. Faintly, a child is crying. As though responding, the child limp in the young couple's arms stirs, flinches, and begins to whimper quietly.

The glowing dots above the receptionist read: CURRENT ESTIMATED WAITING TIME: TWO HOURS.

Starbursts of Kevin's blood have dried on the floor, hardening so that they look like black paint. A man is waiting for the receptionist to come off the phone. She replaces the receiver and turns back to him.

'If you want an X-ray you'd best come back tomorrow, you won't have to wait. Or have a word with your GP.' He seems unable to take in what she says and remains at the counter, gazing at the receptionist, perplexed.

— not very bright. Scared. Maybe something's hurting. Something mysterious; some unspecified, lurking condition making itself felt. What's his problem? His injury?

On the wall a notice in Gujarati, Urdu, Bengali, Hindi, Punjabi and English reads: 'If English is not your first language and you need an interpreter, please ask at the reception desk for help.' The man glances at it without hope: no interpreter on offer for his particular needs. He shifts from one foot to the other. The receptionist sighs.

Outside a siren wails, cut out. The doors are thrust open, attendants fore and aft push in a stretcher trolley. Again for a moment, urgency intrudes, turmoil, as the stretcher is swallowed up by the swing doors. The air slows and stills. Torpor returns.

The stretcher case has a friend who leans on the counter, giving details to the receptionist. 'Where are you from?' she asks, responding to his smile, his bright eyes.

'Turkey,' he says. 'I'm a student.' He has thick, curly hair, beautiful hands, resting on the Reception desk.

'Oh yes. I was in Turkey on holiday once. What're you studying?'

They exchange details, not of the accident, but of their lives; she looks less tired, her mouth smiling. The perplexed man continues to stand by the counter, forgotten. After a few minutes she glances at him, irritated.

'Tomorrow,' she says, 'you won't have to wait. Or see your GP.'

Bridget says, 'Dan? Would you like some tea?'

'Why don't you get yourself one? I'll just have a sip or two.'

She carries the plastic beaker over from the machine and hands it to him. He sips, looks surprised.

'It's sugared.'

'Well, you take sugar.'

'But you don't. It's your tea.'

'Be my guest.'

He gulps, hands her the beaker. She sips, not showing her dislike of the sugary taste, hands it back to him. 'Not bad. Have some more. It'll make you feel better.'

A young Indian doctor strides through the swing doors and pauses. Everyone sits up expectantly, waiting for a number to be called. He heads for the Coke machine and peers at it doubtfully. Puts in a coin, pulls a handle without success. He calls over to the receptionist, his voice languid with exhaustion. 'What do you have to do to get a can out of this thing?'

'Kick it,' Kevin advises.

The doctor raises his eyebrows. 'I don't think so.' He gulps water from a drinking fountain, and is gone, before he can hear the chorus of bleating from the assembled patients and their minders.

Dan says, 'God, he looked tired. Terrible hours, I couldn't take it.' He glances round, studying the other people. Bridget can see him wondering about them, the way he does. She finds herself doing it, noting how the nurses and doctors have grown to resemble one another in their exhaustion, muscles sagging.

– the whole night to get through. And it's our fault, us out here. Waiting for something to happen, waiting to be informed, to be told what the problem is. We've grown to resemble each other, sitting slumped, blank, like plastic mannequins waiting to be put into the shop window, given life and movement by the window dressers. We look numb, bored, try not to show we're frightened –

Kevin stands at the swing doors, face pressed to the porthole, groaning quietly.

'They haven't got the money for staff, you see.' The woman with yellow hair addresses the room. 'Normally we'd go private, but in an emergency . . .' she shrugs. 'Mind you, the nurses are wonderful.'

New arrivals at least break the boredom and everyone watches the two youths, one helping the other, limping in with a black eye and gashed cheek.

'You've been in the wars, then,' says the receptionist.

'This is nothing, you should've seen the Paki.' They

both laugh, one holding his split lip.

The middle-aged couple have been quietly reading, glancing up from time to time to check the electronic panel: CURRENT ESTIMATED WAITING TIME: THREE HOURS. Now, they have finished their books and they start behaving impatiently, shifting in their seats, muttering, glancing at the clock on the wall, then at their watches, as though some mysterious connection between the two has a bearing on the waiting time. Which is the patient? Who has the injury? Bridget wonders. How can you tell?

'It's the stretcher cases. That's the problem. They go to the head of the queue,' the plump woman announces. Kevin begins to pluck distractedly at his dressing.

The couple with the child have been called. The father carries her, the mother stroking her head, murmurs soothingly. The doors swing shut. There is silence, then, from beyond the doors, a high, sharp scream. The screaming goes on, fades into the distance.

Suddenly no one looks bored. Couples move closer, small conversations break out.

Dan says, with contrition, 'Look, you don't have to wait with me —'

'Don't be ridiculous.' She sees that he is in pain, his face pale. There's a small bruise under his eye. Usually he is the one who notices details, she tends to be too busy.

He says, now, 'Well, at least you could have a kip.'

'No chance.'

But she rests her head against his shoulder and drifts uneasily, waking with a jolt to find the nurse standing over them.

'I'll take you through to see the doctor now.'

– how long have we been here? A week? A month? Bridget yawns painfully. Four hours have passed since they arrived.

She sees a slim, sharp-featured woman standing at the Reception desk while a stretcher vanishes through the swing doors bearing a white-faced girl with chewed-looking hair; eyes closed, the lids dark as damsons. She is skeletal, so thin that her body barely disturbs the red blanket.

'I'll just take a few details,' the receptionist says, pen poised. 'Your name?'

'Josephine Marvel, with one l,' the woman says crisply, 'but there's not a lot I can tell you about the girl. I've seen her on the corner near the Underground station. Begging. I found her tonight on the pavement, people were stepping round her, probably thought she was drunk. I couldn't see any bleeding, but –'

'You did the right thing, calling the ambulance. I'll just take a few details . . .'

– what became of the yellow-haired woman? Did they

summon her from the other side of the porthole, and is that good or bad?

Another hour creeps past.

— what are they doing through there? Surely the doctor could just look at him, see it's nothing serious? It can't be anything serious. Maybe he needed an X-ray. But how long does that take? She had an X-ray once when she fell off her bike, and the whole thing took less than half an hour.

— perhaps it's something more. Some internal injury —

The swing doors are pushed open with difficulty and she sees Dan, manoeuvring his way through. She hurries over to him.

'It's OK, nothing broken, just deep bruising.'

'Well, best to be sure.'

'They did an X-ray. Sorry you had to wait.'

They stand there for a moment, uncertain how to handle things. In daylight he might have asked her to drop him off somewhere, he'd be round later for his stuff, but at three in the morning —

Bridget pulls on her coat. 'Come on, I'm dead on my feet, let's go.' She takes his arm. 'You'll need to watch the stairs, in future.'

He drops his head and rubs it against hers, gently, giving or asking for comfort, she's not sure which. Her eyes fill with treacherous tears. She says, 'Come on. Lean on me.'

He says, 'I always do, that's the trouble.'

With the unthinking ease of long practice, they negotiate the steps, her arm holding him, his round her shoulder.

Bolivian Sailors Dream of the Sea

Bolivian Sailors Dream of the Sea

Landlocked. An oddly contradictory phrase, signifying both space and imprisonment. Confined yet open. A landlocked country could stretch no further than itself, knocking its elbows on its boundaries, while a country that melted into ocean breathed air from faraway places.

From the hotel window she could see the twin medieval towers of Bologna, one soaring, spiky; one shorter, leaning towards the other like a drunk engaged in solemn conversation. From the taller of the two, on a clear day, would the ocean be visible? Of course not, yet it seemed to her the coast was never far away in this long boot of a country, washed by two seas from heel to thigh.

This morning they would visit the Morandi museum. They would have lunch somewhere suitable, order tortellini and a fruity Lambrusco, and catch the train to Ravenna for the mosaics. Ravenna had a coastline, albeit marshy. The day was mapped out, as so much of life was, these days. This was both comforting and comfortable. The noise of the traffic grew suddenly louder; beneath her window a motorcycle coughed, grumbling, into life: an advance warning, like the growl in a lion's throat. Then it roared away down the street.

In London, one of her friends had commented on the improved manners of Italian men – 'Remember how infuriating they used to be, Susan? Following us, pinching our bottoms, chatting us up. The feminists must have really got to them, they've changed. No trouble at all.' And she wanted to say: It's not them, dear, it's us. *We* have changed. Thirty years ago we were plump fruit to be squeezed, desired, snatched at. Now, we hang undisturbed on the tree, they don't even see us. And that, too, had a certain comfort to it.

She checked her camera, picked up her bag and sunhat and went out to join Josie for breakfast on the terrace.

The photographer wears a dark suit and a bow tie – even though he's not covering the church ceremony he likes to retain a sense of occasion – not like some of the new boys, with their scruffy jeans and T-shirts. He unpacks the camera case and drapes himself with equipment, garlands of leather hung with steel and glass and plastic: Leica, back-up camera, light-meter. He notices a small, roughened patch on his jacket where the camera has rubbed the fabric. He licks his thumb and smooths it down hopefully. Anyway, no one will notice. Behind the lens he is invisible: nobody looks at the photographer.

Not yet eleven and already the temperature is moving into the high twenties. Tourists stream past, crossing the piazza looking for museums. Locals dawdle, chatting; a few grannies hobble off to Mass. In the centre of the piazza he can see the spray from Neptune's fountain catching the light like a rainbow. The sound of the water is tantalising: he becomes aware he's thirsty. He glances up at the mermaids riding their dolphins, fingers cupping breasts, encouraging water to spurt from nipples. Whoever heard of mermaids with two tails? Very unlikely. He stuffs rolls of film into his pockets, wipes his face with a clean handkerchief and takes a breather.

He falls into the usual ritual: check film, polish lens, complain. Why do all these people want to get married? And why do so many of them want to get married on Sunday? And have pictures to remember the big day by when they're old and grey. Possibly divided by death or acrimony. Why get married at all? It's not compulsory. Yet here they are, forever marrying one another. On the other hand: give thanks, he has a living to earn.

Couples are already lining up outside the Town Hall, the girls in white, the men in stiff collars. Some are chattering, elated, some nervous. One or two are already showing signs of impatience or irritation which could be a problem before long, in his experience. The guests hang about, laughing, as they always do. Most of them are wearing the sort of clothes that only see the light of day at weddings, christenings and First Communions. He'll be doing the usual camouflage job when he takes the group shots, covering up the disaster areas – 'Let's see your lovely smile, signora,' he'll say to the bride's mother, manoeuvring her into flattering obscurity behind a conveniently flowing frock.

A busker has set up shop on the other side of the Piazza Maggiore. Loud. The amplified beat hammers at the photographer's head; he feels bruised, and flags for a moment, his mind a blank. Overhead the sky is a hard, cloudless blue that hurts the eyes, a blue as unnatural as a tourist postcard. He prefers the sky at sunrise, pearly, like the frosted glass of the light-box in his studio. The softer light would do most of these girls a favour: the harsh sun shows up every line and flaw. His shots will need retouching, later. He checks the clock: the next pair should be out any second; time to polish the lens again. Dust everywhere.

The first job wasn't too bad: the bride wore a nice dress, and the skirt swung out like a drooping lily when she sat sideways on the cross-bar of their bicycle. That's what they wanted: a shot of the two of them on the old bike, pedalling off into the future. Simple pleasures. Sweet, really. So he did it. They circled round slowly, in their finery, while he snapped away. Cheek to cheek across the handlebars. Then they got into a big, chauffeur-driven car and glided off while one of the guests took care of the bike. The camera never lies.

Already time for the next pair: he catches them coming down the steps and out into the square, guests cheering, throwing rose petals. Pretty girl, what's-her-name? He checks his notebook: it helps if you remember their names, makes it personal. Maria Theresa. Slim. Dark. Nice dress, they're all nice dresses, but you can see this one's well made, she knows someone, or her mother did it, fits well, good fabric. The bridegroom on the other hand –

The photographer curses silently and with relish: it will be hard to get this one looking good. The hairdo reminds him of Liberace, plus the outfit's the colour of mint toothpaste, that chewing-gum green, suit, shirt, waistcoat, tie, even the socks. And the hair, bouffant, lacquered, with cunning little curls teased onto his forehead. Disaster. The photographer signals encouragingly to the bride, calling out her name, creating an atmosphere of consequence, a sense of celebration. It all helps, gives the eyes a sparkle, otherwise they go dead. He wipes his face, licks dry lips. To work.

Susan leans from the museum window, watching the pattern of sunlight and shadow in the crowded piazza.

Outside the Town Hall a bride and groom pose for photographs. The two huge squares dwarf the crowds within them; the palaces standing shoulder to shoulder, the extravagance of pilasters, balustrades, stone filigree, staircases and statue-studded façades simmer in the heat, stone seeming to melt in the haze. There is a busker at one side, flanked by mobile amplifiers, the music from his electric guitar floating up to the window, coiling round her, heady as incense. Young music. She watches him move, the lithe body, mass of golden curls, strong neck. Young men with similar features look down from museum and cathedral walls all over the country, standing in for the Archangel Gabriel in numberless Annunciations: the same blue eyes, bright hair, open, unmarked face. But the busker wears leather jeans, he lacks wings and his movements are far from spiritual. She feels unsettled, oddly low-spirited, and when she mentions this, Josie suggests it might be to do with the paintings around them on the walls: the muted Morandi palette, 'All those beige bottles and glasses. You've been spoiled by the *quattrocento* extravagance.'

Susan glances through the next window and sees that a circle has formed round the busker, girls and boys moving to the beat, some squatting on the shallow steps of the basilica, one or two dancing on the spot. She too would like to dance, to shake her branches in the sun, but

choices shrink, she has found that. She is – technically –
free to do anything. In fact . . . like being landlocked, she
is at once free and held in. She turns away and follows
Josie down the wide marble stairs.

Maria Theresa stands obediently where the photographer has positioned her, the bouquet held low, 'to
reveal your slim waist', as he put it. The dress is tight, but
not too tight. She breathes easily, waiting. She notices
that the photographer is breathing heavily, wheezing a
little, frowning. Next to her Franco is also being
arranged, his arm holding hers, body turned slightly
sideways. The suit was a bit of a shock – he wanted it to
be a surprise, he said. There's an open-work broderie
anglaise border just above the hem of the jacket, she's
never seen anything like it before, and hopes she never
will again. The jacket is short, cut rather wide. It makes
Franco look shorter. Shorter and fatter. Could he have
put on weight? She'll need to watch that. Put him on a
diet. She always knew she was taller than him but he
seems even shorter today. It must be the jacket.

She becomes aware that across the square a musician
is playing electric guitar. The wave of music surges
across the open space and she feels the impact somewhere below her ribs, vibrating in her thighs, her
breasts. The musician wears black leather trousers,

tight, with no shirt. His bare chest gleams in the sun. His skin, a little lighter than the terracotta wall behind him, is wet, slicked with a sheen of sweat. She can smell his acrid armpits. She can't, of course, he's too far away, but she senses the animal smell, the matted hair. The photographer is asking them to move on, he needs another background. Obediently they cross the square, the music louder now.

She glances again at Franco's suit. Made specially for the occasion. She still can't believe that lacy border. And the green, like pistachio ice-cream – no, she saw a bathroom suite that colour once in a magazine, the whole set, bath, toilet, bidet, basin. That exact pale green. It makes his face look yellow. They could always get the suit dyed later; it would take a dark brown quite well. She'll have to talk to him.

The photographer is beckoning, he wants them in front of the fountain. Franco tells her to pick up the hem of her dress, better for the picture, and to keep it clean – there's grime and muck everywhere. She looks up at the mermaids on the fountain, the way they flaunt themselves, fingers squeezing nipples, scaly thighs gripping the dolphins beneath them. The music pulsates, louder, the musician's leather-clad loins are pressed tight against the guitar; he moves, pelvis rocking, driving the rhythm, face rapt, eyes closed . . . She moves closer; now she can see the slight stubble on his cheeks. When he hits a final chord on the guitar his body arches – 'One more shot!' the photographer calls out, aware too late that the bride's mouth had sagged open unflatteringly as the shutter clicked. The next pose does it: serious; questioning. Nice. Not your usual bride shot, though. Not one for the shop window.

Friends are laughing, someone pats her on the shoulder, shouting jokey advice into her ear. Franco hands her into the waiting car, still worried that her hem might get dusty. The car is air-conditioned, cool, the leather seats immaculate. She seats herself carefully, arranging the skirt round her satin shoes. Franco gets in after her, trying to avoid creasing his pale green trousers. The door slams shut, cutting off the music, though she can still see the musician, guitar swinging, foot tapping to the beat. Inside the car the engine hums quietly. The door to the world of dust, sweat, noise, gusto and passion has closed. Maria Theresa looks out through the tinted glass window as the car drives off. She looks back. For a moment she thinks she can still hear the music.

The photographer winds on the film, re-loads, wipes his face on a large handkerchief. Fine linen; you can't wipe your face on those paper tissues, not properly. Lucia always complained about the handkerchiefs when they were first married: I'm the one that has to wash them, it's the ironing that takes the time. There's enough to do already, with the shirts, and everything else, she used to tell him. And he would reply that his mother never complained about his father's shirts. Wives aren't what they were, he used to say.

A coffee in the shade of the arcades. A charge of caffeine. Soothed by the illusion of coolness, Susan feels better already, out of range of the sunlight that splinters blindingly against the stone columns. The sound of the guitar filters through the crowd and the busker is briefly visible as people shift and move apart, rearranging their pattern. Had she made other decisions, taken other paths, she might have had a son about that age, looking perhaps not unlike that boy: she as a girl had been golden, until time devalued her and plated her hair with silver. She finds herself dreaming as she rarely does, about the other, alternative country she might have inhabited, one circumscribed by domestic ties and small, uncelebrated satisfactions. But also with terrors, dangers, anxieties that did not diminish with the years.

After breakfast, Josie had written postcards to her daughters. This must happen a lot: women outlive men. All over the place, in picturesque settings, widows are busy writing home, having a wonderful time, wish you were here, to offspring unlikely to echo the sentiment. Susan had filled the time reading about an archaeological expedition in Bolivia: an attempt to prove that the land-locked altiplano high in the Andes was the site of the drowned city of Atlantis. The vast plateau was once an inland sea, its lakes still hold mysteries. From time to time lost treasure is unearthed; why not Atlantis? The expedition was setting out with experts from various interested – and affluent – countries. They would play archaeological games, testing the descriptions from ancient writings against the visible landscape, exploring the terrain, attempting to navigate the twisting water-ways on woven reed boats, heading for the Atlantic. And to help them, a detachment of that contradictory force: the navy of a landlocked country, men who normally spend their time patrolling lakes and rivers, and dreaming of the sea.

The photographer checks his notebook. Four down, four to go. Another couple to freeze for eternity. This girl's a worrier. The plain, nice groom fiddles with his tight collar, gently pats her wrist. She is drained, pale from tension. Relax, the photographer tells her, I take care of things here and my partner will be waiting for you at the other end, at the reception. We've never lost a wedding couple yet. That one usually gets a laugh. Not today. She's too tense. All the guests are on a city bus, rented for the occasion, decorated with white ribbon rosettes. In from the suburbs for the celebration. They get off the bus, line up for a huge wedding group, he hates this kind of thing, just like a school photograph – half of them will have their eyes shut and someone will be picking his nose. The bride's acne is showing through the make-up. Now all the guests are filing back on the bus, and the photographer asks her to get up onto the platform for a shot with her friends.

As she steps up, she sees, above the heads of the crowd, two women, English tourists by the look of them, one in a loose cotton dress and flat sandals, the other in designer jeans, with a big, soft leather handbag over her shoulder. Unseen by the two women, a muscular local youth is trailing them, his eyes on the handbag. The second woman pauses to check her camera, and the boy makes his move: picking up speed he overtakes the sandal-clad one, and reaches out for the handbag slung so temptingly from the other woman's shoulder. The bride wants to cry out, to warn them, but she's too far away. And in any case, the floral frock has woken up to the danger. She breaks into a run, swings her camera on the end of its strap, the leather case curves in the air and brushes the thief's shoulder, knocking him off course, the handbag tantalisingly out of reach. As he races off into the crowd, he pauses to send a volley of abuse at the two dazed women, jabbing his index finger skywards.

The photographer is calling, anxious to get his shot. The bride, still watching the pickpocket, sees him trip on a paving stone, sprawling at the feet of passers-by. He is scrambling to his feet as the Englishwoman's camera case arcs towards him – and connects with the dark curly head. His outraged yell of astonishment and pain floats across the piazza and the bride throws back her head and breaks into laughter, tension forgotten, radiant, as the shutter clicks. The photographer can hardly believe his luck. When the pages turn, when grandchildren pore over the album, laughing at the outmoded fashions, they will exclaim in admiration. Caught at that moment on her wedding day, she will be forever beautiful. And he's got the perfect shot to put in the window. The groom pushes her affectionately into her seat and they all drive off, laughing.

The photographer reloads his camera, five down, three to go. He reaches for a handkerchief. He'll be washing it out tonight, with the others, hanging them to drip dry over the bath. He has not yet learned how to iron. He always thinks about Lucia when he's doing the handkerchiefs. He still misses her.

Reunion in Ooty

Reunion in Ooty

Everything was different – even the name – now officially Udhagamandalam, though no one used it. Old India hands returning on nostalgia trips found to their dismay that Ootacamund was not what it had been. True, in the leafy churchyard the gravestone to the bishop ('A labourer and overseer in that portion of the Lord's vineyard planted in India') still stood reassuringly in place, firm and upright; but in town the streets were pot-holed, the gutters piled with rubbish and *filmi* music crackled and wailed from speakers at every corner. Shop doorways were draped with tinsel and adorned with plastic models of favourite deities set dancing by the breeze. Regular water shortages afflicted the shoddy new hotels. The genteel Englishness had worn away with the years. Ooty had become just another bit of Tamil Nadu.

But the Blue Mountain railway still chugged up through the hills carrying refugees from the scorching summer; the downs rolled gently, the streams wound their way past the clumps of trees. And as the weather grew fiercer down on the plains, Ootacamund cast its cool lure. The Nilgiri mountains shimmered with a blue as vivid as memory. Indian families travelled up from Hyderabad, Madras and Bangalore, escaping the heat as the British once did; stately, sari-clad mothers, fathers pausing to take snapshots of the children – boys in Lacoste T-shirts, girls with jasmine threaded through their plaits. They looked in on the Gothic splendour of the Nilgiri Library to leaf through *The Times of India* or *The Hindu*, those who noticed amused to see a mahogany-framed Queen Victoria still hanging on the wall.

Dharam Singh and Mrs Singh, exploring the Botanical Gardens, paused to consider a rather assertive floral display and he caught the eye of a tall, pale English girl in crumpled shorts, holding a camera.

'I wonder if you could take my picture?'

He focused, clicked the shutter, handed her back the camera with a smile.

'You were in Ooty before?'

'No, but I've heard about it. One of my mother's friends was born here –'

'Really!'

'Well, not right here, Delhi I mean –'

'Ah yes. The Raj and all that. Nice to have you back – as visitors!'

They parted company, she in search of a cheap curry in town while they headed for one of Ooty's surviving clubs. By the gates, two small girls joined hands and spun giddily, giggling, their full skirts swinging out like lotus buds, brilliant against the green of the grass.

Mr Singh looked about him with a comfortable sense of well-being. Delhi never gave him this pleasure. He still remembered his first experience of the big city, fifty years before, his father pulling medical strings to get him a consultation with a specialist. He recalled his sense of anxiety, the feeling of being trapped in streets seething with traffic, assaulted by noise from all around, afraid of being late for their appointment. There had been an incident. The rickshaw carrying him and his father had almost run into a sacred bullock emerging lethargically from a side street. The rickshaw had in fact bumped the beast, causing it to quicken its pace, and a big black car coming the other way, chauffeur-driven and carrying some English people, had swerved to avoid a collision and gone head-on into a city bus. There had been a screeching of metal. Blood. People screaming. And then the rickshaw wallah had swung them off, down the nearest turning, nervous of getting involved. Not that it was his fault: sacred cows were a menace on the street, Mr Singh's father had declared, soothing the frightened man.

'That's Delhi for you,' Mr Singh said aloud.

Mrs Singh gave him an incurious glance. They had been married a long time.

Poised above the town, the club garden stepped its way up the hillside; lawns, flowerbeds, trees well placed to offer shade, with the clubhouse, a low sprawl of a building, straddling the spine of the hill, its veranda foaming with fuchsias in hanging baskets, geraniums and nasturtiums in pots, as it had in the old days. People sat, dotted about in garden chairs, enjoying the misty view; or strolled among the flowerbeds.

Mr Singh carried on slowly up the winding drive. Below him, on a half-saucer of lawn curving out over the hillside, his wife had paused for a rest on one of the wooden benches. The benches could seat three, four at a pinch, but her ample flesh and flowing sari turned the simple seat into a throne. She sat, composed, glancing about with occasional turnings of the head, bird-like, enquiring. Her expression was placid. Her husband would have been surprised by the violence of her thoughts: resentment that her daughter-in-law was too busy with her designing career to give enough attention to her family; anxiety about her older son's health: did all lawyers work so hard? And the grandson, spoiled, neglected, wasting his education making videos to encourage the doomed aspirations of the poor. Inwardly, Mrs Singh churned.

At seventy Mr Singh was fit, but he mistrusted excessive exercise. All this nonsense the young went in for with gyms and machines. He paused now, to catch his breath, and at the same time admire a flowerbed, each bloom poised at the moment of perfection, before the shift towards droop and decay. He noticed, coming up the hill behind him, a tall, thin Englishman of about his own age, wearing a sports jacket. Mr Singh's light grey suit, the perfect weight for the mild day, had been made in Savile Row and his shirt not far away in Jermyn Street. He caught the Englishman's eye and called out, 'Someone's keeping a sharp eye on the gardener. Prizewinners here.'

They fell into step, the Englishman slowing his stride. 'You're visiting?' he asked.

'From London,' Mr Singh explained. 'We were in Delhi for a few days. We were supposed to be here last year for Independence Day anniversary celebrations but the mood hardly seemed right. I said to them: what is so special about fifty years? Is India fifty years old? Rather more than that I think. To be frank, isn't it merely the anniversary of a departure?'

He paused.

The Englishman said, 'Oh, quite. And how did you find Delhi?'

'You know, Delhi is becoming altogether impossible!'

Mr Singh flung up his hands. 'My son lives in a very pleasant little corner, private road, gated security, all the rest of it, but in two years three residents have been done to death – murdered – would you credit that?'

'Good God! Has anyone been charged?'

'My dear fellow, of course they have. It's the staff every time. The householders are at the mercy of their servants. It puts one in mind of that play by Jean Genet!' He glanced at the Englishman, but the faded blue eyes mirrored no complicity; the allusion had fallen on stony ground.

'You've lost me, I'm afraid.'

'You're not a theatre-goer then?'

'Here? Hardly. There used to be a touring Gilbert and Sullivan company that dropped in now and then, but –'

'You're a resident!' exclaimed Mr Singh.

'We stayed on, yes.'

Introductions were effected: Mr Singh shook hands with Mr Chadwick. They walked on.

'And your first name?'

'Um, Derek.' Mr Chadwick disliked the modern fashion for moving with immoderate haste on to first-name terms, but Mr Singh took no such step towards intimacy.

'You know, I remember these gardens,' Mr Singh said, glancing around. 'I was here once, as a kid. It hasn't changed at all.'

'Oh, it's not what it was, I'm afraid.'

'No?' Mr Singh cocked his head enquiringly. 'In what way?'

'Well, the membership, of course, is –' Mr Chadwick stopped, embarrassed, conscious of a gaffe yawning at his feet. But his companion had not, it seemed, followed the thread of the sentence. All was well.

Mr Singh gazed dreamily out over the surrounding hills with their blue shimmer. A faint smell of eucalyptus hung in the air, sharp, cleansing.

Mr Chadwick gave a little cough. 'The membership is – much bigger, it's lost the intimacy, the . . .'

'Exclusivity?'

'That's it.'

'Democratisation, Chadwick. Quite unstoppable. Look at Eastern Europe.' Mr Singh gave an amused shrug. 'So you stayed on. And your family?'

'My wife's been Home once or twice to see our son in London, but . . . we've been here too long. She couldn't get on with things there. She felt a stranger. Graffiti everywhere. And all the muggings –'

'That depends on where you go. We have a very pleasant abode in Ealing. Leafy suburb they call it. No ruffians there. The streets are impeccable. No winos or dog's business fouling the pavement.'

Mr Chadwick had no views on Ealing, past or present;

for him life had been boarding school, then back to the family tea plantation two hillsides away. The world had spun and parts of it had broken up, but his corner had stayed much the same. Adjustments had been necessary, of course. After Independence.

'You'll find Ooty is much changed,' he said. 'Rackety new hotels, traffic all over the place, windows full of fax machines and computers –'

'Ah! Information technology. My area of activity, I won't hear a word against it. My lawyer son is of the opinion e-mail is the greatest thing since Gutenberg.' He breathed in the scented air and exhaled with satisfaction. 'Your son works in London then: doing well, I trust?'

Mr Chadwick did not reply. He bent down to deadhead a bloom in one of the intricately shaped beds, plucked at a weed or two, and the conversation dwindled away.

Mr Singh looked up at the sun, glanced at his watch and announced that he was peckish.

'Look here, why not join me for lunch?'

Mr Chadwick shook his head regretfully. 'Much as I'd like to . . . but in any case, I'm afraid it's members only. They're pretty strict –'

Mr Singh patted his arm reassuringly. 'No problem, old boy.'

'You're a *member?*' Mr Chadwick sounded incredulous. 'But –'

'– But I'm not a resident? Isn't it? Well, let's say I like to keep in touch. And a distant cousin of mine has connections. So. Shall it be lunch?'

Mr Chadwick seemed uncertain of his response. He slapped his pockets as though searching for some small, elusive object, and smiled without mirth. 'In point of fact,' he said, 'I am – in a sense – on duty. On call, you might say. A bit tricky.'

Mr Singh raised his eyebrows and waited; his expression expectant.

Mr Chadwick attempted lightness, amusement, 'I – um – manage the place, d'you see.'

Mr Singh looked impressed. 'You're the *burra sahib*, eh! Well, good for you.' He added innocently, 'An Englishman running things. They don't mind? Your Indian members?'

Searching for words, Mr Chadwick creaked his way to explaining that as to *running* things, there was of course a General Manager in overall charge. 'I'm more in a day-to-day capacity.'

'The invaluable General Factotum, eh?' laughed Mr Singh cheerily, but Mr Chadwick failed to share the joke. He gave another of his coughs. 'I'm not really in a position to – ah – enjoy myself.'

'We'll see about that,' said Mr Singh, and steered him up the steps, onto the veranda and into the clubhouse. 'I'm giving you lunch. Member's rights.'

'I really don't think –' Mr Chadwick began, but Mr Singh was guiding him to the dining room and Mr Singh was murmuring to the head waiter and one palm brushed against another. Without a blink the visitor and, by extension, Mr Chadwick, were seated at an excellent table near the window flanked by a burgeoning potted palm.

Mr Singh studied the menu.

'By the way, we've met before,' he said, his eyes scrolling the dishes of the day.

'Oh? Surely not.'

'Mm. More than fifty years ago. I was just a kid, you weren't much more – helping your father I seem to recall –'

Mr Singh beckoned over a waiter and ordered a beer. He went on studying the menu until the drink arrived, and then sipped it appreciatively.

Mr Chadwick licked his dry lips. The waiter had failed to bring one for him.

On the hills that folded and curved beyond the clubhouse window, the old bungalows of the British were visible here and there, but now saris fluttered in the gardens, drying in the breeze.

Mr Singh said thoughtfully, 'I contemplated buying one of those – matter of sentiment you know, "a local habitation and a name" –' but his companion had stopped listening: a man at a table across the room was glancing about impatiently and tapping his fork against his water glass. Mr Chadwick signalled to a waiter with an urgent jerk of the head, eyebrows eloquent.

'Never off duty, eh?' Mr Singh murmured. 'No rest for the wicked.' He picked up his beer. 'Where's yours? Good lord! The silly fellow forgot to bring you one. Letting club standards down!' He called for another beer.

'Great days, Chadwick. Great days. We knew the British were on the way out. We were itching to get our plans on the road but things dragged on, those last years. My father was a schoolteacher, education was his passion, we were fed Eng. Lit. with our mother's milk, but by then Independence was all he could think about. They held meetings, he and his cronies, full of grand ideas, and one day some of the younger ones decided to march on the club. I tagged along. I was a music student, the *tabla*, you know, but we were all politicos then. We picketed the premises –' he glanced out of the window. 'It was one of those damp, misty days, a chill in the air ... There we were, chanting away for Home Rule. It was what you'd call a demo now, but everyone was jittery; the club members decided it was a riot.'

Mr Chadwick wiped his face with a handkerchief. 'I'd forgotten,' he said.

'Well . . . easily done. After all: so many Indians, one can't remember them all, can one? Ah, here's your beer.'

'I meant the riot – the demonstration. I believe the police . . . over-reacted,' Mr Chadwick muttered.

'They certainly followed instructions to the letter,' Mr Singh remarked. 'Laid into us with their *lathis*. I recall someone yelling "Teach the blighters a lesson they won't forget!" I think that was you, Chadwick old man. Yes, that was you. Well, heat of battle and all that.'

'I don't recall –'

'I do. I'll say one thing: if the British bobby had been supplied with *lathis* instead of truncheons, there would have been a lot less trouble with those student demos in London. Six feet of solid wood, brass-tipped at the business end . . .'

He was gazing out of the window again. He smoothed back a lock of grey hair.

'They broke my fingers.'

He regarded his misshapen hands impassively.

Mr Chadwick glanced and looked away, quickly.

'Terrible,' he said, conscious that something more was needed but unable to find the words. 'Terrible,' he repeated.

'Oh well,' Mr Singh said cheerfully, 'it's an ill wind, as

they say. No more music. But I would probably have made a mediocre *tabla* player and ended my days poor as a church mouse. I turned out to be something of a whizz at business. So you could say you fellows did me a favour, eh?' He roared with laughter.

Across the room, the waiter had failed to placate the unhappy member. Mr Chadwick excused himself hurriedly and went to investigate.

'One chicken and one lamb, I ordered,' the small man in the Nehru jacket said irritably. 'He brings two lamb. Then the fellow takes away one lamb and brings this –' he prodded at his plate with one finger. 'What is this object? This is not chicken!' Mr Chadwick apologised, sent the waiter scurrying, apologised again. He returned, somewhat red in the face, to find Mr Singh standing at the window, waving at someone.

'My wife!' he exclaimed impatiently. 'She seems to have decided to opt for lunch after all. I'd better fetch her in.'

Mrs Singh approached the steps of the veranda and turned to say goodbye to the frail Englishwoman who had been showing her the gardens. 'It was nice talking to you,' Mrs Singh said. 'We all have our problems, no?' She touched the other woman's arm. 'I hope things go well for your family.'

Sybil Chadwick, whose high-heeled, ankle-strapped sandals had skimmed the parquet floor of the ballroom like a spinning top, whose white throat had filled with laughter at fancy dress parties and picnics long ago, drooped in her floral frock, the once porcelain complexion as wrinkled as a dead rose. She watched the other woman make her way up the shallow steps, undulating comfortably, like a silk-wrapped walrus.

A grey-haired Indian came out onto the veranda, followed by Sybil's husband, slapping absently at his pockets. She heard Derek explaining that lunch was not really something he went in for, he had duties, things that needed attending to, he hoped Mr Singh would forgive him –'

'– Don't give it another thought, old boy. My dear wife will keep me company, she talks enough for three. And look here, thanks for all you've done.'

'I haven't done anything –' Mr Chadwick was saying as Mr Singh shook his hand warmly, pressing folded paper into his palm.

Sybil Chadwick, waiting at the foot of the steps, saw her husband's face stiffen, grow pale. He stood frozen as the Singhs went on, into the clubhouse. He came down the steps and held out his hand, showing her a wad of notes.

'He gave me a tip. A tip.'

His skin seemed to have shrivelled so that the bones

of his face stood out, giving it a skull-like look.

Behind him, visible through the open archway, the embalmed heads of animals shot long ago by club members gazed down from their wooden shields. His blue eyes, like theirs, had a glassy blankness; a lifelike glitter, not the thing itself.

For a moment she was tempted to sympathise, to try to minimise the shame. But then she thought of her middle-aged son sinking into a torpor of redundancy in London, a grandson getting by as a brickie in Dubai, and she was filled with a savage resentment against Derek for all he had done or failed to do, long ago.

'Good,' she said, lethally cool, 'it'll come in handy. You should see if you can pick up a few more.'

She turned away from him, rubbing at her eyes, and sniffed quickly.

'Sybil?'

'I'm all right,' she said. She fished out her handkerchief and blew her nose. 'It must be the eucalyptus.'

She gazed out at the view sent Home on all those sepia picture postcards. On the lawns far below, children chased each other, slender gold necklaces glinting in the sun; a young man talked earnestly into his mobile phone; a father clicked his camera. In town they were setting off fire-crackers and from the open-air cinema there came the sound of distant cheering.

Body Blue

———————

Body Blue

She walked nonchalantly into the formroom, late for class, the others already at their desks. There was instant uproar: cheers, whistles, the whoops of encouragement they had learned from TV game shows. The teacher banged on the table, attempting to regain control. Rocky was dazzling to the eye, broad blue stripes daubed on arms, legs and neck. Branded with indigo. Exotic as a zebra.

The noise filtered through the walls of the staff room like a roar from a distant football pitch. 'What the hell's going on now?'

'Oh, someone's probably been knifed. We'll get to hear.' Curiosity was deferred. Instant coffee was sugared and stirred.

She had begun behaving badly at the start of summer term; rowdy in class, bunking off into truancy, and when she did appear, defying the rules with a rag-bag of clownish outfits – baggy trousers, a grandfather shirt with cuffs that covered the knuckles, heavy-duty boots. A provocative statement, on the face of it, but the teachers were puzzled. Rocky was not a troublemaker, good things were expected of her; rare among her peers, she participated: she had won a local competition with a painting of 'Where I Went on my Holidays'. The judges had been impressed and put it on a poster. But now . . .

'She's at that age . . . thirteen, isn't she? They sometimes need to demonstrate independence.' So: turn a blind eye, see how things go?

May brought a heatwave, and as the temperature rose, Rocky abandoned first the boots, then the trousers, and by the second week was back in a cotton dress.

Things seemed to be going well. No one could have forecast the body paint.

The news spread through the school in waves, beginning at the gates, through the playground, into the hall, up the stairs and, late as usual, into the staff common-room.

'She's wearing body paint.'

'Where?'

'All over.'

'Actually, it's beautiful in a surreal sort of way,' said Davis, in charge of Art.

Surreal, possibly. But unacceptable. She was sent for.

'Right, what's all this, then?' Miss Lennard kept her voice muted, enquiring.

'Body paint, miss.'

'Yes.' A pause. 'Why?'

'Traditional. It's the approach of the solstice. Ancient Britons –'

'Rocky: in this part of London I don't think you'll find a lot of solstice celebration going on.'

'You let the Hindus and Muslims have their festivals, they celebrate Diwali and that. Why –'

'It will have to come off. You must remove it.'

The girl shook her head very slightly. 'I can't do that.'

Miss Lennard's voice rose – to her dismay, she heard a strident note creep in.

'You refuse?'

'No. But I can't remove it.' She added helpfully, 'I expect it'll fade with time.'

Should she be sent home? Suspended until the colour wore off? Exams were looming; she was expected to do well. And these days, with league tables and general uncertainty, a school needed all the points it could get. Miss Lennard felt exhaustion creep over her, weighting her limbs. It became harder, the fight. She tapped her desk with a briskness she did not feel, and suggested a compromise: if Rocky wore tights and a long-sleeved blouse they would allow her to attend school.

Meanwhile, she was queen for a day. Boys, uncertain, sniggered, but girls admired the sinuous bands of blue that spiralled her arms. coiled up her legs like tame snakes, circled her neck, bold as tribal decorations.

Sandra, who sat next to her, offered admiration – 'I really love it, Rocks. Wish I had the nerve.'

Rocks, generally known as Rocky, christened Roxanne, said in her neutral way, 'It's no big deal. Some of the tarts round our way put more stuff than this on just their face.'

Davis in charge of Art caught up with her in the corridor. 'It's Matisse blue!' He smiled encouragingly. 'Remember that painting you did for the competition? The beach and blue sea? And now, what you're ... wearing. It's the same blue as the background to Matisse's *La Dance* ...'

She looked at him silently until his eyes flickered and he moved on, remembering he was due for a class.

When she walked home, cars swerved, horns hooted. An old woman shook her head and made disapproving noises involving teeth and tongue. On a building site, workers called down from scaffolding perches, 'Circus in town, then?' and, 'You an advert, darling? What you selling?'

The crumbling Victorian terrace sat on the cusp of respectability, between Portobello Road and no-man's-land. The house fronts were pocked and flaking, their cracked windowpanes reinforced with sticky tape and cardboard. The pavements were veneered with a mixture of abandoned Chinese takeaways, dribbles of milk from broken bottles and starbursts of ancient vomit, trodden in and flattened to abstraction, hardened to a lasting sheen. In the road, shreds of soiled paper fluttered in the hot breeze, attempting to fly free of sticky tarmac. At the windows of grim, narrow houses, net curtains sagged, heavy with grime and dust, some drooping unevenly from their rails. Number 7 was no different from its neighbours.

She climbed the chipped steps and turned the key. Locked from the inside, the door stayed shut. The paintwork was faded and blistered and for a moment or two she stood popping the brittle bubbles, rubbing the crumbled paint between her fingers. Then she sat down on the top step and watched the passers-by: a red-faced man carrying a plastic shopping bag that chinked, bottle against bottle, as he went past: a Rastafarian in knitted beret and designer trainers, walking jauntily, tripping to a rhythm only he could hear. An elderly man walking his dog. The two progressed slowly, the dog pausing at every lamp-post and gate, quivering with interest, swiftly cocking a leg, the man waiting, patient. The breeze, gritty, thick with exhaust fumes, detached a torn sheet of newsprint from the gutter and it hung an instant in the air before whirling away, a severed headline – 'CRISIS IN –' keeping its geographical secret.

At the other end of the long street two houses had

recently been done up: cracks repaired, brickwork painted a flat, tasteful grey. Claw-footed baths and bidets had been delivered; pale blinds masked the windows. The front doors had the same deep, many-coated lustre as the new owners' cars parked outside, inviting broken windows and theft.

Rocky had seen them admiring their homes; sleek young couples bright with confidence and money. One of them said it was certainly a mixed neighbourhood, 'but on the way up', which made it sound as though the houses were built on an escalator. Well, maybe things were moving, at the top end; but number 7 was at the bottom of the street, and unlikely, in Rocky's opinion, to rise.

She shifted down a step, glanced back at the house behind her. The windows were closed, the rooms dark behind sagging grey net. The sun shafted through a gap between two buildings, glittering on bits of broken glass strewn across the street. She closed her eyes and sat waiting. Through closed lids she felt the warmth of the sun bathing her face, and remembered a moment from a long-ago holiday when her father had lifted her onto his shoulders and walked into the sea, beating his chest and roaring triumphantly. Shrieking with pleasurable fear she had screwed up her eyes against the brilliance of the sun, the sea inching up her legs like cool silk as he went deeper into the indigo-blue water. He used to play around all the time, growling, 'Me Tarzan, you Jane' to her mother, or chasing the child, a make-believe monster who held no menace.

They had driven to the seaside in the camper van he bought from some Australians who were going home. 'Good van, this,' he said that day, patting the steering wheel, 'take you anywhere. Fancy North Africa?' They had all laughed, but perhaps he had been serious, because not long after that he went off in the van one day and didn't come back. There had been many occasions, since, when she closed her eyes tight, shutting out the world, making a wish, praying for this or that. Waiting.

She thought about the places the van might have taken him; warm places with the smell of spices and the murmur of foreign tongues.

There was a clicking of the lock and Rocky's mother opened the front door. 'Come on, then,' she said, and slapped away down the dingy hall wrapped in a stained and skimpy peignoir, the edges of which had once been trimmed with fluffy pink. She looked back and paused.

'Get into the kitchen and wash that stuff off. He's in a good mood, what d'you want to upset him for?'

Somewhere a door banged and a moment or two later a toilet flushed. The woman and the child stood silently in the dark hall. The uncarpeted stairs creaked loudly as the man came down from the floor above, clearing his throat.

At the kitchen sink Rocky sluiced her arms and face with water, cool as silk, silky as the cool sea washing her legs. It was Sandra who had told her, years ago, about some Hollywood star who kept her silk stockings in the freezer.

When her mother got married again, Rocky was maid of honour, required to wear a pink dress that rendered her hot with embarrassment. Her mother wore pink and off-white – 'Strawberries and cream,' she said, laughing, 'naughty but nice.' Rocky asked for silk stockings as a special treat, to wear at the wedding, and her mother bought her a pair of nylons, pale and slippery as condoms. Rocky put them in the fridge. On the morning of the wedding she was fishing them out when he came in, already wearing his best dark suit.

'What's that?'

'Stockings –'

The laugh-lines left his face like creases ironed from a shirt. 'In the fridge? That's not nice. That's disgusting. You'll have to be chastised for that.'

She looked all right at the wedding; she found her mother's blemish concealer and put some on her face and nobody noticed anything. She did not wear the new stockings: he had burnt them, out in the back yard. Let that be a lesson to her, he said.

On the day Rocky appeared at school in stripes, Miss Lennard went to a dinner party, invited by a woman she had known since university. Most of the other guests seemed to be success figures, a journalist, an advertising man, a woman who analysed TV commercials for semiotic significance. Esther Lennard was aware that her contribution to the evening was inadequate; her life was stressful but dull. She drank her wine and listened.

Across the table a dark-haired woman entertained the table with her latest family problem; a rebellious teenage daughter: 'It began with a stud in her nose and now it's fluorescent orange hair –'

Miss Lennard poured herself some more wine. A stud in the nose. How quaint. And orange hair. Her own problems included scissor-fights and drug-pushing in the playground, but nothing new there to offer the table.

She said, 'Today a girl came to school in blue body paint. Striped.'

'Tell us more!' someone said.

There had been pictures taken at the wedding, and Rocky brought one to school. Sandra looked at the laughing group, the happy couple, the maid of honour in her pink dress, her face turned away from the camera. She studied the dark-suited bridegroom.

'He looks OK,' Sandra said. 'Has he got a job?'

'He works on an oil rig.'

'What, North Sea? He must go off for ages then.' One thought leading to another, she asked, 'What happened to your dad?'

Rocky shifted her shoulders in a dismissive shrug, gave a don't-ask-me tilt of the head.

One day he was there, then gone. Scarpered. Her mother cried for a bit, then she put on a bright red mouth, pulled on a tight frock and went out. In time, another razor occupied the cluttered bathroom shelf, another body moved into the double bed.

'D'you call him Dad?' Sandra asked.

'I don't call him anything.'

When Rocky came in next day, Davis in charge of Art waved a magazine at her. 'Look: Matisse. *La Dance.* Early version, 1910. There's that blue, your blue, the background, with the crimson circle of dancers against it. He kept painting that scene over and over, going back to it. Here they are, again, leaping as though their lives depended on it, there's ecstasy, almost desperation there . . .'

She stared down at the picture, the dancers leaping

like flames, the blue surging behind them. He said, 'You can borrow it if you want.' He turned the pages.

'See how the later versions became paler, the blue fading, the figures drained of colour, almost transparent, as though they were dancing themselves out of existence. Here –' he held out the magazine and patted her shoulder. She flinched, backing away, her face white above the scrolls of blue that circled her neck. There were places where the body paint had almost worn off, or so he thought, until he looked closer. Then he registered the faint purple marks on arms and legs, the weals and mottled bruises that had earlier been covered by the painted stripes.

She took a long time walking home, went slowly up the steps and unlocked the door. In the crackling tension of an impending storm the street was quieter than usual; with a held-in, waiting quality. She climbed the stairs to her room – narrow, cramped, more a corridor than a room really, but it was out of the way and she liked it. On the walls were pages she had torn from the travel pages of Sunday newspapers, with colour illustrations of places she liked the sound of: Zanzibar, Mexico, Madagascar, and Sri Lanka which her father once told her used to be called the Isles of Serendipity. From below she heard shouting, the crash of china, then her mother's voice, high and shrill.

She waited, listening; trying to identify and translate creaks and bangs into actions. A few minutes later there was a thud like a muffled drum as the front door slammed, shaking the house. She pressed her face against the windowpane and saw him go quickly down the steps, almost tripping at the bottom. He strode off without looking back, weighed down by his heavy bag. Rocky watched until he was out of sight, then she went downstairs. Her mother came into the kitchen from the back yard and dropped a box of matches onto the table, brushing dirt off her hands. Her face looked smudged and puffy.

'Best get the place cleared up a bit,' she said, and began to collect broken china from the floor. Outside in the yard, a column of smoke from a small bonfire rose in the still air, coating the leaves of the sickly eucalyptus tree with velvety grey.

'Will he be back?'

'I doubt it.' She threw a broken saucer into the bin. 'I've had enough anyway.' She glanced outside, tension dissolving in a small, triumphant grin. 'And he better not try coming back for that suit of his.'

The heat-wave broke in a thunderstorm that sent rain bouncing off roofs and cascading down house fronts. Gutters flooded, old stains were washed from pavements, and outside the back door of number 7, the deluge battered the smouldering remains of the bonfire. Rocky went outside, her sandals squelching in the puddles. A leather belt with a silver buckle writhed like a snake as it burned. The rain poured down the child's face, drenched her clothes and limbs. Tentatively, not quite knowing how, she began to dance in a circle, round the dead fire and the charred remnants of a dark blue suit.

A Visit to the Zen Gardens

A Visit to the Zen Gardens

She had been one of his students, admiring from afar, keen to absorb all he had to say about sociology and gender, and new perceptions of marginalisation. She watched and listened and noted his lectures assiduously. One day he suggested dinner.

He took her to a curry house and over the bile-bitter coffee he gazed at her, smiling fatuously, and told her she looked like something out of a Renaissance painting.

'You need glasses: I've got no bone structure and my nose is a blob.'

'It's not a blob,' David said, 'it's adorable. You have the face of a cherub, one of those rather wicked *putti* – you know, the –'

'I know what *putti* are,' Connie said. 'Little buggers with wings and fat bums.'

He gave a spurt of surprised laughter, his thin face crumpling into pleasure, his habitual solemnity undermined. This was what she brought to his life: the gift of unseriousness. He did not conceal that he was besotted; he wrote letters filled with jewelled phrases of adoration. He took her on picnics and crowned her red hair with wild flowers; he filled her college pigeonhole with poems, heady stuff, and she capitulated. After that things took a less verbal turn.

On their first visit to his mother in South London, Connie became aware of tension as they approached the small terraced house.

'I thought you said you got on pretty well.'

'Oh we do. But . . . it's not always easy.'

Connie admired the hollyhocks crammed into the space between the gate and the front door. David rang the bell and winced at the musical chimes.

His mother noted the newly acquired tweed sports jacket and woollen tie. 'Bit warm for that, isn't it, Dave?' (Unspoken: what happened to the anorak?)

She was welcoming, comfortable; she offered home-made cake and tinned-salmon sandwiches. David glanced at the tea service and a shadow passed over his face. He picked up one of the cups and examined it wearily.

'What's this?'

'Nice, aren't they? Hand-made in Poland.'

'What happened to the ones I gave you?'

'They're beautiful, Dave. But these are dishwasher safe; I don't have to worry about the colours fading.'

When they left she kissed Connie and hugged her son, enveloping his slight frame in her warm plumpness.

'Don't leave it so long till next time.'

Driving them back to Brighton, Connie said, 'I thought the cups were rather pretty.' He took off his gold-rimmed glasses, held them up to the light and noted a small smear. He polished the lenses.

'She has no taste,' he said.

Over the years many people and places had been judged and found wanting. Friends had failed to measure up, countries had disappointed. David cared so very much about standards that she usually hesitated to cause him distress by departing from the accepted canon. He did not bully, he merely advised: 'I shouldn't risk that – bound to be second-rate.' And to be second-rate was the unforgivable sin. There had been a time when they had laughed together over disappointments and bad choices. Later, he had learned how to avoid such errors of judgement.

Japan, for David, had long exemplified the ideal environment: a place of delicacy, where less meant more, a living shrine to exquisite taste. 'But you have to know what to see,' he warned. 'It's easy to get it wrong. I want to show you the real Japan.' And now, invited to Tokyo for a symposium – 'Blueprint for the next Millennium?' – he would make sure the real Japan was what she saw.

It was at Narita airport, as they got off the plane, that the accident occurred: a missed step, an awkward stumble, and David was wheeled through Immigration white-faced and bravely British. The fractured ankle was expertly dealt with; sympathetic and soothing, the university officials organised everything: though wheelchair-bound, David would still give his paper: a car would be provided; the delegates would not be deprived of 'The Naked Singularity and the Naked Ape: dread and humiliation in postfeminist sexuality'. A topic perhaps not central to the theme of the conference, but one well-honed by the speaker.

Meanwhile he fretted, helpless: 'I wanted to show you the Zen gardens –'

'I'll be fine. They're laying on a guided tour –'

'Oh, I don't advise going on one of those.'

Next day he and a gleaming wheelchair were driven off to the lecture hall while Connie was left to recover from jet-lag, with a demonstration of flower arrangement threatened for the afternoon. Everyone in London had warned her about Tokyo, a polluted hell-hole of no appeal, but she decided to explore anyway, and wandering down a side-street, away from hotels and skyscrapers, at once found herself in another kind of town: a place of tree-lined back-alleys crammed with tiny houses, sloping-roofed, the porches filled with potted plants. Frail old women in black pyjamas stooped over the greenery, tenderly watering each individual leaf. Between the plants, here and there, a garden gnome stood sentinel. A crocodile of tiny children, identically dressed, solemn-faced, marched obediently behind a teacher. No dawdling. No stragglers. People hurried past, neat, homogeneous, as sharply defined as figures in a woodcut.

She swung back into a main thoroughfare and allowed the crowd to carry her along. Almost imperceptibly it had begun to rain, so softly that no individual drop could be distinguished. A veil of moisture hung in the air, a flocculence through which they all swam, the locals shielded by small, multi-hued umbrellas that lent a carnival swirl to the scene. She was part of a human stream filling the pavement, creating its own current, moving with the choreographed precision of a shoal of fish. She let herself drift, changing direction and pace with the rest; sucked down, as in a dream, into the dark, hot mouth of the subway.

In the train the passengers swayed together, circumspect, each held within a force-field of apartness. Even when elbows inescapably connected with neighbouring bodies there was a discretion about the encounter. A foreigner with bright, frizzy hair, blue eyes and ruddy cheeks, Connie knew she stood out from the rest, oversized and clumsy, her clothes a mess. Seated across the aisle, a girl in a dark, narrowly cut dress nibbled a tiny square of chocolate, then folded the wrapper into a meticulous rectangle and replaced it in her polished leather handbag. Connie stared down at her guidebook and tried without success to make sense of the diagram.

She turned to the man seated next to her and held out the open book.

'I wonder if you could help me with this?'

He flinched, avoiding eye contact, blinking rapidly, and stared down at the page.

'I'm afraid I'm quite lost,' she added.

Reluctantly he touched one of the black lines with a neatly manicured finger.

'We are here.'

'The hotel said there was a place I could buy a kimono. For my daughter.'

A pause.

'Ah.' Hesitation. More rapid blinking. 'Such places are maybe not easy for you to find.'

'Oh.' Connie waited, then sighed. 'She'll be disappointed.'

He cleared his throat, swallowed, coughed again. 'Near my work, is pretty good shop.'

A pause.

'Yes?'

'Er. Maybe there you can find something . . .'

She beamed and patted his arm. 'Wonderful! Thank you!'

He looked about her own age, forty perhaps. Speaking slowly, the words creaking out, he asked if she found her holiday enjoyable.

'Oh, it's not really a holiday –'

'Ah! Working trip.' He nodded.

'There's a sort of conference –'

'Ah! And –' pause 'er – your job . . .'

Connie briefly pondered an answer. David had been insistent that she should give up her course when they moved in together. It was ethically indefensible that he should be shacked up with one of his students. Once safely married, she could go back to college, but the children arrived before she had got round to planning for them and she never went back. Her roles were various: supportive mother; academic wife; caring daughter. She had become a maker of sandwiches at residents' meetings, addresser of envelopes, signer of petitions. But what was all that in the market-place? The girl across the aisle was now reading a glossy magazine with a picture of a designer home on the cover that looked like a concrete mushroom.

Connie sensed him waiting. He had taken the big step, asked a question. He deserved a satisfactory answer.

She said, 'The home is my speciality.'

'Ah! Designer! Perhaps also including the bathroom. Sanitation?' He looked into her eyes for the first time. 'I myself am employed in – ah – toilet factory. Testing and research.'

'Ah!' said Connie. She trawled her experience for comments and came up empty.

They got off at the next station. The kimono shop, he told her, was two streets away. 'Here is my place of work.' She studied the faceless block, touched by the note of pride in his voice.

'It must be very interesting.'

'We have many visitors. Official tours.'

Connie said recklessly, 'You mean I could go in?'

His face brightened. 'Of course! And you will be my guest.'

Mr Kanabe, her new friend, led her round, explaining the science of toilet design and construction, the psychological effects of colour and height, inviting her to feel the heated seats, each equipped with individual temperature control; demonstrating computerised LCD display panels and 'fountain' cleansing jets. And, on special orders, 'massage facility'. He was particularly proud of the testing station. A man in a white coat and brilliant white gloves stood at a conveyor belt while a surreal, apparently endless line of toilet bowls advanced towards him. Into each bowl he launched an imaginatively modelled synthetic turd, followed by an appropriate quantity of tissue, and a measure of bright yellow liquid. 'They will now be tested. Efficient flush-away, etc,' Mr Kanabe said, adding gravely, 'imperfect models will be destroyed.'

'Ah!' said Connie.

When the tour ended he led her back to the entrance and bowed goodbye.

'It has been a pleasure,' he said.

'It has indeed,' Connie said, sincerely. 'You have been very kind.'

She realised she was starving. She wandered past crowded snack-bars piled with chicken wings and bits of giblets on skewers, past sushi restaurants and kiosks serving grilled eels, past *pachinko* gambling parlours with blinding lights and walls of jangling slot machines. Down a side-street, a small room offered noodles, with vividly coloured plastic models of available variations in the window. She went inside and perched at the counter. The place was full and she saw now that she was the only woman in the room. Was she breaking some taboo? No one stared at her, but she had read somewhere that what a Japanese found unpleasing, or unattractive, he overlooked; he literally did not see. Ghost-like, this unaccompanied foreign female was therefore invisible except to the elderly Japanese who took her mimed order for noodle soup. Next to her a man expertly slurped his noodles, managing to fill his mouth without splashing a drop onto his dark suit.

Through the clatter of plates she became aware of a subdued roar, a rumbling vibration not unlike an underground train thundering beneath the floor. The soup lurched in its bowl. The tables shook violently, sliding back and forth drunkenly on the concrete floor. She caught the eye of her neighbour who had replaced his chopsticks neatly on the counter.

'What is it?' Connie asked.

'Earthquake,' he said briskly, wiping his mouth with his napkin.

'What do we do?'

'I think we go now.'

As the floor danced beneath their feet the customers stumbled out into the road. Connie fell against the man in the dark suit and apologised. He said reassuringly, 'It is not such big one. Soon over. But there will be traffic problems I think. Maybe no trains. Are you near to your hotel?'

She told him the name and he frowned. 'Not so near. My wife will receive you until matters are resolved.' He bowed briefly and announced himself: 'T. J. Takanawa.'

Firmly he ushered her ahead of him through the jostling crowd.

David was furious, frantic with worry when she got in. 'We're due at the welcome dinner. You'd better have a quick shower –'

'I had a bath earlier, I'll just change.'

Ten minutes later, she was stepping into a limousine while the wheelchair was stowed in the boot by the chauffeur.

'How was your day?' Connie enquired.

'The usual parochial paper by a Canadian –'

'Wasn't the earthquake amazing?'

'I didn't even know about it till later. The building is quake-proof, apparently. But it must have been frightening for you.'

'Oh, it wasn't too bad.'

He gave her a questioning glance. 'What did you do all day?'

'Well, in the morning . . .'

In the dark interior of the car, the chauffeur's white gloves glowed, luminous. Connie wondered what David would have made of the toilet factory and the testing station. She said, 'I went to a place making . . . um, porcelain things.'

'Oh,' David's voice was dismissive. 'Kyoto is the place for porcelain.'

'After that – well, there was the earthquake of course, and I met a nice Japanese couple . . .'

The block was grey and stark, the apartment tiny. Mr Takanawa took himself off to work while Mrs Takanawa silently made coffee. David had led Connie to expect sliding screens, tatami mats and minimalist austerity; a bit of rare calligraphy on a scroll, perhaps a solitary flower on display – all the restraint that went with Confucian ethics and ancient customs, but the little room was cluttered: a flimsy table and plastic chairs, a stereo, cooker and sink. A shelf held sauce bottles: crimson, brown, black. Mrs Takanawa offered coffee and small red bean-curd cakes.

The silence lengthened, and Connie took a bite of cake. A curious substance filled her mouth, seemingly expanding, down her throat, and into her nose. The taste was indescribable. Mrs Takanawa said, sympathetically, 'Westerners do not always enjoy our food. Maybe more coffee.'

Connie croaked, trying to swallow the bean curd, 'I was hoping to find a kimono for my daughter –'

'Ah!' Mrs Takanawa became animated: 'Kimono or yukata?'

She went into some detail on the difference between

the simple cotton yukata for everyday wear in the home, and the traditional silk kimono stitched from a single length of cloth, which in earlier times had revealed at a glance everything from the financial status to the social class of the wearer. She vanished into the next room and emerged carrying a silken garment patterned in swirls of iridescent green and blue. The colours shimmered like peacock feathers.

'It is for wearing at the wedding of my daughter.'

Connie stroked the silk with a tentative fingertip. 'My daughter –' (why am I saying this?). 'My daughter is what we call a single parent. She's not married.'

'Does this trouble you?'

'I want her to be happy.'

'And your husband?'

David regarded a single parent as an imperfect construct of a family. This created difficulties.

'My husband . . .' she considered her words, truth battling with loyalty.

The limousine was making slow progress. At an intersection, a life-size wooden cut-out of a road-worker waved a jointed arm from which a torch flashed warning signals. Dazzling neon signs winked on and off around them; fugitive rubies, diamonds and emeralds blazed on the soaring walls of the surrounding buildings.

David said to the chauffeur, 'Is it always this bad?'

The man regarded him impassively in the rear-view mirror. 'Oh yes.'

The traffic held them, locked in a line outside a *pachinko* parlour. Connie watched the men, seated shoulder to shoulder, slotting in coins, working the machines.

'Did you find a kimono?'

'I didn't really have time.'

Mrs Takanawa had made more coffee and brought out photographs of her daughter, who was working in London and wanted to marry an English boy, without ceremonial or fuss.

'There was some – difficulty with Father – with Mr Takanawa. Later resolved. It will be a Shinto ceremony.' She added, 'In one of our best *departimentu*. There is a shrine, on the roof.' A Shinto wedding in a department store, Connie thought. Could Harrods match that?

There were other photographs: Mrs Takanawa's own long-ago wedding, showing a childlike figure, the small face painted white, blank as a doll's beneath the white satin head-dress, the small, sad eyes rimmed with red. She, too, she murmured, had wanted her own way in certain matters, but family wishes had been observed.

'In Japan there is a very strong bond between parents

and children. We have a story about the great lion who drops his cub into the valley of a thousand blades. But he does it only to teach the cub to look after himself.'

'I don't like that story,' said Connie.

'I also do not.'

Without warning, tears spilled from Mrs Takanawa's eyes and rolled like pearls down her smooth cheeks. Her expression remained undisturbed, as though a statue wept.

When it was time to go, she accompanied Connie, and they paused outside a department store. Then, without a word, they went inside.

The girls on either side of the lift doors bowed and chanted a welcome in unison. At the rooftop shrine Mrs Takanawa paused beneath a large bronze bell and swung the clapper so that it gave out a hollow clang. She bowed and moved on. By a dark pool in which pink and silver ornamental carp lay gleaming below the surface like ceremonial daggers, she took Connie's hand and studied her palm, charting it with a pale fingernail.

'A good lifeline, see, here, and your fateline is straight. Not like mine. So: you are independent.' Connie began to shake her head and Mrs Takanawa said gnomically, 'Some flowers bloom late in the year. In autumn we have crysanthemums –' the word presented her with difficulties. She repeated it carefully and they laughed together. 'Crysanthemums. Also the maple tree. Gold and red, Emperor's favourite.' Far below them the Tokyo traffic roared softly.

The afternoon session, David said, had gone well. 'That French fool with the puffed-up hairdo tried to hijack the session with his tiresome little talk but luckily I knew where to put the boot in.' She listened while the official limousine inched on, through the choked streets. Somewhere very far away was an empty night sky and darkness. On the rooftops of tall buildings, glittering carp swam in black pools. Down here were crowds and noise and movement. It was as bright as day.

'What else did you do?' David asked.

'I looked in at a department store.'

He sighed.

'Did you know,' Connie murmured, 'that in the ninth century, the ladies at the court of the Emperor were supposed to make sure their kimonos blended with the maple trees? And –'

David said firmly, 'Tomorrow I'll try and organise your day for you. You really mustn't waste this opportunity.'

After leaving Mrs Takanawa, Connie had wandered for a while. When she began to feel unwell she looked about for somewhere to sit down, but the neighbourhood had changed: she was surrounded by small office buildings and anonymous-looking shops with shuttered frontages. Hot, shaky and nauseous, she was uncomfortably aware of losing consciousness as she keeled over into the arms of a surprised young man emerging from a doorway.

When she came to, she was lying on a folded futon in a bare, concrete-floored room with boarded-up windows. Around the walls shelves were stacked high with shoe boxes. More boxes were piled on a battered table, and still more filled a packing case beneath it. Two young men stood watching her from behind wrap-around dark glasses. As she sat up, one of them hastily filled a glass with bottled water, and offered it to her with a bow.

'I'm so sorry! Did I faint? Must be jet-lag. Or bean curd –' Connie was babbling, uncertain at what social level such an encounter should be pitched, when the door burst open and two very large Japanese men in black suits and small black glasses entered precipitously. There was some swift and violent movement, involving punches to the stomach and a brief flashing of a blade, before the visitors kicked over the table, up-ended the packing case and energetically swept the shelves bare. Then they were gone, leaving the room awash in cardboard boxes and mismatched footwear, the floor heaped with trainers of extravagant design, flaunting world-famous logos. Connie's rescuer and his colleague writhed, groaning, on the floor. Throughout, huddled on the futon, Connie had been ignored: here too, the foreign body did not exist.

Coughing and retching, the pair fumbled for the dark glasses which had been knocked flying in the altercation, and replaced them carefully, while blood flowed from their slashed cheeks, splashing the trainers nearest to them. They surveyed the trainer mountain, moaning softly, ignoring their injuries.

'Shouldn't we call the police?' Dazed with shock, Connie sounded unnaturally calm.

But the police, it seemed, were not required: this was a private business matter, a misunderstanding about distribution arrangements. Briskly they began to sort the shoes into pairs.

'Well,' she said, feeling redundant, 'perhaps you could just point me in the direction of a taxi . . .'

Dinner, organised by the university, was an exquisite affair. Colour, flavour; the container and the thing contained, all were calculated, matched, arranged. David murmured 'visual genius' like an invocation. Connie felt she wasn't quite up to the catering. She studied the guests seated at the long table, impassive as the men she had seen earlier in the gambling parlours. Mr Kanabe had told her he called in every day after work. It was good for stress, he said, and there was always the possibility of the big win, the jackpot.

The meal was almost over. Waitresses in kimono and wooden sandals moved from guest to guest with tiny, hobbling steps, handing out hot towels. Connie held the scalding cloth to her face, closed her eyes and breathed in the smell of steaming fabric.

Earlier, when they had said goodbye, Mrs Takanawa had mentioned the Japanese tradition of the *sento*, the public bath. 'Maybe you should try.' Connie had been doubtful, but when she got back to the hotel, dusty, sweaty and slightly spattered with bloodstains, she realised her appearance might cause some distress to David. She paused at the marble and steel reception desk and asked where the nearest public bath might be found.

'Lower ground floor, madam,' the clerk said. 'Just give room number.'

In the outer chamber of the baths, women seated on tiny plastic stools vigorously soaped and sluiced themselves. Connie, too, scrubbed away the day's grime and stress.

The public bath, big as a swimming pool, shimmered with heat. Voices were muted by the rushing of a cascade, through which came the sound of giggling, the birdlike calls of one woman to another while they bathed, their bodies smooth and pale as peeled almonds, their perfect torsos and short legs hardly concealed by the tiny hand towel the size of a face flannel each modestly held before her when entering the pool, the atmosphere an unlikely blend of seraglio and boarding school.

Once, soon after they were married, she and David had attended a seminar held at an obscure American university where they were introduced to the pleasures of the hot tub. There, beneath the stars, with a bottle of Californian champagne and plastic glasses, they had luxuriated in the flesh, the giddy abandonment of the body to bubbling water, warm night air and slippery intimacy. He had called her his mermaid but her strong, brown legs had trapped his pale body in a grip no fishy temptress could match.

Like mermaids, the Japanese women rose from the water bare-breasted, the blue water blurring the distinction between fishtail and legs. The glimmering reflections of the water wavered on the blue-white surface of the marble walls. The world was washed away and Connie rested, floating in the liberating warmth of steam and water.

The evening was not yet finished: the dinner guests were herded politely to a private view of the latest work by a highly regarded Japanese artist and Connie found herself next to one of the American delegates, tanned, silver-haired and well-preserved in the style familiar from television soaps. He immediately introduced himself and beckoned over a couple from across the room.

'Two fellow-Brits for you. Let's see: John and – Josie, right?'

Connie glanced at the pair, looked again at the dark, slim wife.

'Jo? It is, isn't it?'

Pause. Recognition. Exclamations of pleasure and surprise.

'I'm here with David,' Connie said.

Another pause. 'Of course.'

No need to say more. No need to remind themselves that Jo had advised against, warned, cautioned, offering her opinion that sequestration in a closed order would be preferable to life with David. She had not attended the wedding. They had not kept in touch. Indeed, their last encounter had been bitter.

The husband – 'You haven't met John' – a tall man unexpectedly gentle in his manner, smiled, cupping his wife's elbow affectionately.

'Did you have problems with the earthquake?'

'No, I met some people. They were kind: she made me coffee. And read my palm.'

'They're rather keen on that,' John said, 'but it's a woman thing, I think. No one's offered to read mine.'

'I could tell you what I've learned,' Connie offered, seizing an excuse to fill a socially hazardous moment. She took his hand, brushing the warm, smooth palm with her fingers. 'Here's your fateline, just like mine, shows you're independent, and here –' she paused, disconcerted, at a loss how to proceed, for the lifeline she was tracing with her finger ran out, stopped short, not at all resembling her own. He smiled down at her, encouragingly, waiting. 'Yes?'

She shook her head, relinquishing his hand.

'I've forgotten the rest.'

She felt Jo's eyes on her, questioning; sensed a qualm, a sinking of the heart, and she said to her old friend, 'We should meet. Shall we?'

'Yes.'

The American, studying the work of art before them, was remarking on the difference between Oriental and Western art. 'We regard what they do as unfathomable; they conceal, they hold us at the surface, unrevealing.'

'And what do we do?'

'Oh, we reveal ourselves. "Who am I?" we ask. "What are we?" The history of Western art is a quest for the self, the revelation of the creative subjectivity of man.'

Connie caught her friend's sideways, sceptical look, an expression she remembered well. She thought of Mrs Takanawa, and teardrops on the smooth cheek; of dark-suited young men, the planes of their cheeks scarred with a flashing blade; of *pachinko* parlours manned by impassive, hopeful Rumpelstiltskins. And of a lifeline ending abruptly. She said aloud, 'I think the surface also reveals the self.'

'Ah, you're quoting the modern philosophers, I see!' the American exclaimed, and turned to David who had been wheeled up to them. 'Your wife is quite an East-West analyst, professor.'

David looked regretful. 'Hardly. I'm afraid she has had no chance at all to get to know Japan. My fault, this silly business of my ankle. I wanted to show her the Zen gardens. It's been rather a wasted trip for her.'

The French Wedding

The French Wedding

The *notaire* had informed her that, according to French law, she could now sell the house without paying a franc of capital gains tax. After twenty-two years, the profit was deemed to be amortised.

Amortisation. (OED) 1. The extinction of a debt. 2. To deaden or droop.

Amort. In the state of death, without spirit.

How perfectly judged. She could now, if desired, without penalty shed a possession that had outlived its value and its life. There had, in any case, already been penalties enough. Those years lay heavily on her. She felt . . . spiritless. Could a person be amortised?

Josie became aware that she had driven too long in silence, lost in thought. She owed it to her passenger, her friend, to offer conversation.

'The really boring thing about the French,' she said, 'is that they always manage to wrong-foot you. Invitations, for example –'

The car breasted a rise and before them the hillside dropped gently into the valley, fold after fold of vineyards, catching the late afternoon sun. The vineyards created their own imperatives, rows of vines marched up the fields in close formation, deep, inky shadows running like open trenches alongside. It was a landscape of order and symmetry, no unruly elements permitted. Josie, raking it with a resentful eye, found it altogether too neat. Vines should riot; here, they were tamed into submission. True, there were pockets of resistance in the fields: nature fighting back; wild flowers exploding cheekily, scattering brilliance across the monochrome fields. A few frail, spear-sharp trees lurked on the skyline flashing subversive signals when the sun caught the metal of their leaves. Josie welcomed the rebels; the life-force was not to be regimented without a struggle, thank God. She saluted an insubordinate sunflower, self-seeded from another year's crop, bright head raised above a sea of green.

'Lovely, isn't it,' she said flatly, statement, not question. She changed gear and drove on before Susan could reply.

'Invitations, for example,' she repeated. 'They invite you for an *un apéritif* at seven and you think, well that'll be a drink before they eat, you don't want to keep them hanging about. So you arrive on time and no one else turns up for another half-hour and it goes on till midnight.'

'Well –'

'Next time you're invited, you think you know the form, so you arrive twenty minutes late, and you find a roomful of people already there, clearly wondering what kept you. You cannot get it right. With the French.'

'Even after all these years?'

'Even after all these years.'

It was different at the beginning of course, when she was newly arrived, eager to learn, moved and astonished by the 'otherness' of France –

The landscape blurred suddenly into a haze of Impressionist light and shade as tears pricked her eyes. Too many memories, too many journeys.

That first time, when she had looked about with innocent eyes, noting the precise geometry of the plantations, she had exclaimed, bewildered, 'These can't be vineyards!' She remembered Bible readings at schools, where someone or other was forever 'walking in his vineyard'. She had pictured them as romantic, shady places, the vines criss-crossing overhead, heavy with fruit, fragrant.

These were waist-high leafy walls, efficiently tethered to industrial-strength wire supports. No romance at all.

Exploring, she and John had noticed a small red rose-bush planted at the end of each row of vines. They had been charmed by the detail, so aesthetically pleasing.

'Later we found out why they were there: roses are

more susceptible to disease than vines, so if the rose sickened, it provided an early-warning system.'

'Very practical,' Susan said.

'Very French.'

Well, not entirely, Susan reflected, thinking of canaries down coalmines, but she decided the comment would be unwelcome. She felt increasingly uncomfortable. She had known the trip would be nostalgic; she had feared it might be sad. She had not supposed it would be embittered. If the place brought on this reaction, why, then, were they here?

As though reading her thoughts Josie said, 'This wedding. It's going to be ghastly, of course. But at least I'll be able to check the septic tank and have a look at the roof, see if the tiles are still in place.' And set in motion certain actions too long delayed. 'I'm glad you came,' she added. 'You'll keep me sane.'

Susan was beginning to wonder whether this brief holiday might have been a mistake. She was unaware that her companion, too, was wondering the same thing.

But sooner or later Josie would have had to make the trip: this place, once the repository of Arcadian dreams, had become a burden she no longer needed to support. Time to cut the cord.

Without John the house seemed less attractive, the drive tedious, the problems more frequent. She had come to realise that in truth the place had been more his than theirs. He had repaired the cracked windowpanes, dug the holes for plants, dealt with the leaking roof. He had enjoyed spending three weeks whitewashing walls, woodworming beams and killing nettles. Without his central presence the house became redundant; the girls regarded it as too remote and preferred to go backpacking with friends. Josie, too, reneged: she found that a cruise of Greek island classical sites or the Pharaonic treasures of the Nile Valley gave her more pleasure than filling her carrier bags in the local market and eating a solitary salade Niçoise at a rickety garden table, reading the local edition of the *Sud-Ouest* and batting away the wasps. Increasingly she lent the house to friends in return for the odd spot of maintenance and grass cutting.

As yet another summer came and went she would write the regretful letter to the French neighbours – 'Not this year after all, alas,' and pay the water rates, the *taxe foncière* and *taxe d'habitation*. Or non-habitation, as it now more often was.

Then the invitation had dropped onto her London doormat. She stared at the silver bells and satin decorations and pushed the card away from her, to the lower end of the kitchen table where unanswered letters and junk mail nested. But the wedding of Béatrice and Stéphane could not easily be ignored.

When they bought the house, she and John, not long married, still felt like students. Buying the French place – 'so cheap, honestly, you couldn't get a car for that at home' – was part of a game, a toe dipped in the dream of faraway. In London they had a rented flat; in France they were landowners. 'Two *hectares!* We could grow fruit. Vegetables. Plant a few vines. It's wine country, after all.'

The neighbours were *vignerons*, their wives – some without the benefit of running water in the kitchen – preserved plums in eau de vie, killed their own ducks and chickens and made crêpes as delicate as lace. Béatrice and Stéphane were babies, still unweaned, encountered with their respective parents on market days or at village festivities, each summer.

Susan yawned. Green and brown striped landscape flashed past the windows; mile upon mile of vineyards. The regularity of it was hypnotic. She said sleepily, 'You used to get so irritated when people called it your place in the Dordogne –'

'Well it's not. It's the Gironde. It's Aquitaine, it's the Sud-Ouest, it's Entre-Deux-Mers. Not bloody Dordogneshire.'

'I've always liked that idea, of a land between two seas, between the Atlantic and the Med.'

'That's what we thought too,' Josie said, 'until the

neighbours put us right: "Between two *rivers*, actually, madame: *Entre la Garonne et la Dordogne.*" Wrong-footed again, you see.'

Still, with time, Josie and John had built up friend-ships that survived the unnatural, stop-go rhythm of annual visits. The vegetables had remained a fantasy, but there were years when they picked their own plums, cherries and apples. London friends, speeding down from Paris on the TGV, envied them their French con-nection.

Josie introduced the locals to blackberry crumble, made from the brambles permitted to flourish on the land belonging to *les Anglais*. They attended cele-brations, and hosted some. They had seen the local infants grow into children; kept pace with the opera-tions, illnesses, gossip and feuds, the ups and downs that marked all their lives. Meanwhile *les Anglais* produced the girls: Flora, Allegra and Vee, short for Primavera, three pale, quiet babies who grew into pale, languorous beauties in the swan-necked, Botticelli mould.

There had been an occasional funeral notification, a black-edged letter giving news of a departed matriarch or an uncle, met once or twice. Next visit the loss would be explored with easy, consoling tears (on the French side) and (on the English) an equally comforting aware-ness that this was something that happened to other people. Their own final reckoning lay a long lifetime ahead.

And then John died.

'Nearly home,' Josie said. 'We can pick up supplies here.'

The town that had once seemed so romantic was now just a place to replenish the larder, more valued for its *alimentation* than its architecture. Sleepy in the late-morning heat, the medieval houses lined the narrow street, half-timbered fronts bleached by time and sun, overhanging gables shading the pavements. Around the market square deep, vaulted arcades hunched their stone shoulders against the intruder. This was one of the *bastides*, the walled towns that formed the dowry of Eleanor of Aquitaine, bitterly disputed, fought over, first French, then English, then French again.

At the beginning Josie and John did their shopping at Madame's in the village: a one-room general store with smoked hams and salamis hanging from the ceiling, vast slabs of Gruyère on the counter, local melons stored on the tiled floor to keep them cool, rope-soled espadrilles stacked up on shelves alongside fancy corkscrews, rat poison, fly-killer, cheap wine-glasses in dusty boxes of six . . .

In those days, every Friday a van drove in, and

dropped its side wall to reveal a marine display glittering like a jeweller's shop window: silver sardines, grey and pink shrimps, mussels gleaming like jet; mullet bright as coral. For the squeamish foreigners, other displays were less appealing: live eels squirming in a tub and the alarming bloody bulk of tuna to be sliced into. At noon the *poissonier* closed up and drove away to his own waiting lunch.

Down by the river, at the mill, the baker used to rise halfway through the night to work on his dough and feed the huge wood ovens. Like everyone else, Josie and John called in for long sticks of bread still hot from baking, breaking off bits to nibble on the way home, pausing at the cramped little bar for a Pernod.

Now the *hypermarché* at the crossroads outside town had everything the global village dweller might need, from feta cheese to Thai green curry paste. Sliced bread. Instant coffee. Housewives stacked up their trolleys with pre-packed portions of cheese, chicken drumsticks and frozen *quenelles*. Packet soups. The miller had retired. Madame's had closed. As had the bar. Instead, the villagers stayed home, their rooms lit by the flickering blue glow from the television screen, the fields and vineyards beyond their walls obscured by the beaches of southern California or Texas skyscrapers.

'Nearly there,' Josie said again. A last slog up the

bumpy country road, past a château sufficiently crumbling to be classified as picturesque, bought by some Parisians and done up as a summer residence. Since her last trip, Josie noted, they had put in steel-framed patio doors to the barn and built a gas-fired brick barbecue.

She turned left, across a field of maize. One year they had arrived to find it planted with sunflowers, upright and blazing. By the end of summer the petals had withered; the dark faces drooping on their shrivelled stems like a defeated army burnt and blackened on the field of battle, a doomed battalion waiting to be scythed. Odd how this peaceful landscape always inspired in her images of carnage and death. Was it the old battles, the buried, rusting instruments of war, the restless bones under the rich soil? Or more recent conflicts, the bitterness of World War Two, the line drawn through the land, marking off the Occupied from the Unoccupied sectors, dividing a nation more fundamentally than mere barbed wire or concrete wall. There had been butchery here, less than sixty years before, Resistance forays, women and children murdered in Nazi reprisals; families sundered, loyalties betrayed. Hostility, buried like old bones, persisted; there were *froideurs* for which no explanation was needed, outbreaks of abuse at sensitive times of the year, when war memorials were decorated and old medals worn. Late summer could be disquieting, with those blackened warriors staring sightlessly from the fields.

She sent the car curving round a last bend and the house came into view down a winding side-road, lying tucked against the slope of the hill, its long roof of weathered terracotta tiles sloping from the attic above the front door down over the adjoining barns to end no more than three feet from the ground.

An empty house, a few trees, a wire fence marked 'Propriétée Privée'. Not a lot to show for twenty-two years.

'It's beautiful,' Susan said loyally, though in truth it was an unpicturesque, four-square stone farmhouse of little visual appeal. She wondered why they had bought this one and not, for example, the house further up the road, which had an old *pigeonnier*, or the one they had driven past earlier, with its sheltered, creeper-clad courtyard and slender turrets.

'John loved it,' Josie said, as though answering the question, 'because it was so plain. No pretensions, no look-at-me charm.' And of course, no neighbours living on your doorstep. The nearest house a quarter of a mile or more away, beyond the fields. But nobody could have guessed that to be an advantage: John was always so welcoming, pulling out a chair for the unexpected visitor, offering a glass of something, enquiring about expectations of a good *récolte*, or problems that might arise from the latest Bordeaux scandal.

It was going to be hard to break the news to their French friends. How best to do it? The approach direct: 'I've decided to sell.' The devious: 'There are problems: I may have to . . .' Or the diplomatic untruth: 'No alternative, I fear . . .' And when? Not at the wedding. But suppose a casual question came her way, an enquiry about her plans, what then? Perhaps she should have stayed away and sent a letter.

Josie unlocked the front door, using two big steel keys and a Yale. Inside, the house was more spacious than Susan had expected, and cool, even on a day as hot as this. It smelled of damp stone and wood-smoke and had the waiting stillness of a place left empty for too long.

Susan carried in the supplies, Josie went from room to room opening shutters, letting in the light, as she always did, as she had done that first day, though then she had exclaimed in wonder at the way the sun glittered on the dried-up grass outside the window, turning the straw to gold. Now she left that to Susan. She switched on the electricity and put white wine and mineral water in the fridge – 'First things first.' Then she pulled the polythene sheets off the furniture. 'Let's see what the mice and moths have managed between them.' Later she would check the roof for dislodged tiles, see if pipes had frozen in the winter, if cracks in the walls had widened. The joys of ownership. In due course she would show Susan the local attractions: the fourteenth-century abbey, the watermill, the prettiest riverside restaurant in the whole *département*. The usual stuff. They had explored it all together, she and John, year by year.

And, now, everywhere she went, he was there, imposing himself by his very absence; the brush of his hand against hers as she walked down to the woods at the bottom of their land; the bang of a shutter or the half-heard sound of a voice across the field calling up his presence. When she looked ahead, up the sun-bleached road wavering in the heat-haze, she all but caught sight of him. Turning, she thought she saw him, lingering to examine a flower growing at the side of the path, almost palpably there. That half-smile, that tilt of the head –

'Go out to lunch tomorrow, shall we?' she suggested briskly. 'Try a Michelin red *repas* place.'

Susan, as a guest, hardly liked to say that it might be nicer just to stay here, in the shade of the two vast lime tress, and read.

And again there was that uncanny response from Josie, as though the words had been spoken aloud: 'We hardly ever went out to eat. John so relished being here, the silence. So different from London, and the office, phones ringing, faxes spilling out. That's why we never put in a phone. Of course, it did mean driving up to the call-box at the crossroads with a fistful of small change when we needed to contact anyone . . .' She shrugged and laughed. 'So eating out is a treat.'

And Susan had her treat too, later, when they carried chairs out to what Josie mockingly referred to as the west terrace ('All this was rough grass with old bits of farm machinery lying about when we got it'), sipped the local white and watched the sun disappear behind the dark smudge of hills on the horizon, birds noisily bedding down in the trees, until imperceptibly, silence crept over the landscape and even the cicadas were stilled. For a long time afterwards the sky stayed deep crimson, gradually fading to dusty pink, to grey, then indigo as an invisible paintbrush spread wash after wash across the heavens. When it was dark the silence was broken by a sudden, questioning oboe note, and then a full, answering chorus from the frogs down by the pond. The moon swam up behind the trees, and they went inside and lit a fire; more to enjoy the flickering logs than for warmth.

In the night, Susan woke to the sound of rain pattering on the tiles, loud, like insistent knocking. Gathering strength, the drops swelled to a downpour, battering the roof. She opened the shutters and leaned out, raising her face to the rain that fell like a curtain, blotting out sky and stars. The steady deluge, the water roaring loud as a cataract, the sense of a vast, inundated landscape, sucked her back into childhood: wrapped comfortingly in her ayah's shawl she squatted on a marble-floored veranda trying to see through the massed needles of the monsoon rain falling so close that occasionally one hit her nose, making her flinch and laugh.

The needles tingled now on her skull. If only they could pierce the skin, shaft through to the brain so that the black blood of memory bubbled up, frothing, scum-like, leaving empty holes to be filled by rainwater. A brain filled with rainwater, cleansed of memory, regrets, useless feelings, what an improvement that could be. A raindrop bounced now on her nose. She wiped it away and went back to bed.

'What do you wear to a French wedding?' Susan had asked, alarmed, when she discovered the invitation had been extended to include her. This, after all, was a formal occasion. She would need a hat. Proper shoes. Gloves?

She assembled a collection of garments and took a pitiless look at herself: a large woman in an unfortunate floral print frock topped by a ridiculous hat. An Osbert Lancaster cartoon of a Home Counties matron dressed for an Occasion. Perfect. She packed the lot.

On the day of the wedding she ironed the dress on a corner of the kitchen table and prepared to suffer. She could, of course, have avoided all this, the embarrassment and the agony. She could have said no thanks, and stayed behind at the house, enjoying some local cheeses and, later, a nice cup of tea, still drinkable even with long-life milk.

But one couldn't be ungracious, could one? And in any case, Josie, an unaccompanied woman among all those Gallic couples and family groupings, needed a supportive friend. So she put on the tights and slip and frock, and made up her face and brushed her hair and pinned on the hat and fished out the good leather handbag that made her feel like the Queen, and hung it over her arm and said brightly, 'Will I do?'

'Perfect,' Josie said mechanically, before she looked up and registered the outfit, and then it was too late to say anything. 'Absolutely fine,' she amended. And what did it matter anyway, here? Who would there be to impress?

Josie had wrapped the wedding presents: English porcelain for the bridal couple; a bottle of single malt for the groom's father; Tiptree's Little Scarlet for the mother – the only English jam the locals acknowledged as a contender in the *conserves* stakes.

The drive to the groom's father's house took fifteen

sweltering minutes through silent, deserted vineyards. The green battalions flashed past them, row after row, heavy with fruit, stretching out to the horizon, an immaculate study in perspective. Ripe pears hung, bright as Christmas tree baubles against dark leaves. And through the open windows of the car, over the rise and fall of the land, she could hear the cicadas signalling one to another with their creaking, endless susurration. It was not a sound Josie cherished. There were times, she thought, when it could drive you mad.

'Bloody cicadas,' she said aloud, 'you can't get away from them.'

'Darwin said he could hear them as he stood on the deck of the *Beagle* a quarter of a mile from the shore.'

'Well, poor sod, then. I'm surprised he got off the boat.'

By the roadside a magpie was about to win a tug-of-war with an unlucky worm. High overhead, a hawk cruising lazily, made a sudden dive from the sky to pick up some lunch – a field mouse, a small rabbit – and a faint scream of terror drifted on the breeze as he lifted off, talons curved round a small bundle that squirmed and then hung still. In this empty land there was, Josie decided bleakly, no room for the idle spectator; the whole of nature was a fight to the death: eat or be eaten. Fulham was gentler.

'I'm afraid there's always rather a gauntlet to run on arrival,' she warned Susan. 'They'll be lined up ceremonially to greet me and meet you. Handshakes, and you have to *faire les bises*, do the kissing, left cheek, right cheek, it's a bit of a strain, being the focus of all that attention.' And of course there would be questions.

She swung the car through the farm gates and almost ran down two men, dashing across their path, flapping arms and shouting. There seemed to be about a dozen people in the yard, all chasing a huge pink pig.

'Just a moment!' one of them called out in French. 'We have to get this beast back where he belongs.' Waving, shouting, they danced about, heading off the pig, herding him towards his enclosure while the visitors hung back, trying not to get in their way.

Susan watched the scene, the balletic figures, the men with slicked-down hair, wearing Sunday-best that came out of the *armoire* only on occasions like this, suits of blue or bright tan, and shirts with ties; the women in floral-print frocks or polyester two-pieces. All running improbably about a farmyard trying to corner a pig. There was mud and there were puddles; polished shoes were at risk here. But even as she watched, the fugitive was recaptured and they all turned to greet the Englishwomen.

'*Joséphine!* Welcome! Such a long time!' Ceremonial

kisses. They turned, paused, then, politely, to Susan. 'Does she understand French, your friend?'

Nobody attempted English, though one or two of the younger generation could have done so. The groom, for example.

'Stéphane's English is excellent,' Josie said encouragingly. 'The girls helped him with his homework when they were all so-high.'

He was dark-jowled and awkward in a slightly too-large dinner jacket and wing-collared, starched shirt. He kissed Josie warmly on both cheeks and shook hands with Susan while assuring her – in French – that she was very welcome, any friend of Mme Marvel's, etc. Susan's French was rusty but she was prepared to try.

'Congratulations!' she began. 'I have heard so much –' but he had already turned away to the next arrival.

'Is that a bad shave or a fashion statement?' Susan asked.

Josie glanced more closely at the groom. 'Designer stubble. Here! How things have changed. I just looked into the kitchen: a young mum's defrosting babyfood in the microwave. And they've got one of those ceramic hobs. I remember when they filled buckets from the well over there.'

Friends, neighbours and relatives were presented in

turn. They kissed or shook hands and welcomed the friend from England: 'Does she speak French?'

Susan withdrew into reserve. Here the condition of foreigner and deaf mute seemed synonymous. The groom's father eyed the malt whisky appreciatively; his wife kissed Josie once, twice, three times, exclaiming throatily, 'Without John, it isn't . . .' She wiped her eyes.

There were older brothers and uncles and aunts and cousins and a man from the village with a Zapata moustache and a limp who shook hands formally and hoped fervently that Mme Marvel was in good health and would be staying longer, this year.

Josie waited until the florid welcoming phrases came to an end and he moved on.

'I nearly sued him for trespass once. Him and his bloody sheep, marauding over our fields . . .' She had shouted threats down the phone, reaching for legalistic caveats. And afterwards she had cried, feeling helpless, at the mercy of these Cartesian rationalists whose actions were so transparently guided by self-interest. While she, in the vulnerable position of foreigner, summer resident, bird of passage, lurched between the defensive and the ingratiating, they simply demonstrated the ruthlessness of natural law.

'Ah, these nostalgic memories,' she said, without affection.

When more guests had arrived, fruit squash was produced. Swallowing grenadine with water, Susan longed for wine, better still a cold beer – even a shandy would have been preferable to this sickly syrup. Her face ached from keeping a perpetual smile in place. Josie's minimal make-up had disappeared under the onslaught of all the ritual kissing, her cheeks rouged from the blurred lipstick of others. For a moment they stood alone.

Susan murmured, 'They call you Joséphine.'

'They're disinclined to get their tongues round foreign-seeming names. Josie would never have done. I would have been Mme Marvel for ever if John hadn't suggested Joséphine. It gave me a sort of historical credibility.' She glanced surreptitiously at her watch. 'Thank God: I see a ground swell developing.'

They all surged towards the cars, which the older children had been decorating with silver and white silk rosettes and streamers. The cavalcade moved off to collect the bride, blasting through the country lanes and hamlets like an invading column, trailing dust and cacophony, the drivers leaning on their horns.

Susan had attended few weddings over the years: a friend or two, a colleague in her teaching days, and that was about it. Nothing special. She had forgotten, until the car hooters re-awakened the memory, her very first wedding, when she was five, in Delhi; an affair of marigold garlands and sweetmeats studded with pistachio nuts; of tinsel decorations glittering in the sun. There had been a procession, whistles and hooters loud in the street, male guests and musicians accompanying the groom; and in an upstairs room a silent bride with downcast eyes seated with the women, their saris shimmering with gold thread, and she, a child, an outsider, permitted to sink into the velvet cushions and stare at the jewels winking from the shadows, admire the pearls and jasmine woven in the bride's black hair. After a while she had been sent home in the car with the driver, her parents to follow later. Childish memory is an unstable recording machine: she recalled clearly the tinsel in the sunlight, the intricate henna patterns painted on the palms of the bride's hands, but could not recall her mother's face that day, odd, since that was the last time she saw it. The accident had happened on their way home, a local bus, travelling too fast, swerving to avoid a sacred bullock, crushing the car, the chauffeur and her parents –

'Are you all right?' Josie asked. 'You look a bit pale.'

'The heat,' Susan explained. Trapped by the windscreen wipers, a silver and white ribbon rosette caught the sun, glittering, bright.

'Does she speak French, your friend?'

The bride was dressed in white floor-length silk. On

her short blonde hair she wore a circle of dark purple flowers. ('At least they match the roots,' Josie commented later to Susan.)

'You've changed your hair.'

Béatrice shrugged philosophically. 'Maman's idea. She thought a blonde bride would go better with the dress.'

She shook Susan's hand briefly and moved on.

'The bride doesn't seem very excited about it all,' Susan commented.

'Well they've been living together quite comfortably for four years, so it's hardly a leap in the dark.'

'So why now?'

'Oh, for the family of course.'

'When do we get a drink?'

'Not yet.' Josie's damp fringe was stuck to her brow. There was a sheen of perspiration round her eyes and upper lip. She grimaced ruefully. 'They feel it's rather gross, the way the English thrust alcohol into a guest's hand as soon as he puts his head through the door. They're much more delicate.'

Susan found a patch of shade under a tree and thought longingly of the gross habits of the English. A glass in the hand was worth two in the more delicate offing. At last the signal was given and they all moved on.

Cars. *La Mairie*. Witnesses. Mayor in tricolor sash. Questions and answers. Signature.

Susan had given up on the smiling; her tongue felt swollen, filling her mouth. Her lips were cracked and dry and her palms felt greasy, her handbag strap bit into her arm, sweat collecting in the ridge it formed. Her straw hat, which had seemed so sensible, had grown increasingly tight, her forehead throbbing beneath the pressure. Far from providing shade, it seemed to be trapping the heat so that her head felt boiled.

The clock struck three and the wedding party poured out into the sunlight. The air inside the car smelled of burnt plastic, the seat too hot to touch.

'Halfway there,' Josie said grimly.

The church door was decked with an arch of feathery branches; inside, family and friends had been busy: the flagstones were carpeted with a chequerboard of leaves – laurel and box – laid out in perfect squares that led from the entrance to the altar. Susan could see, in a distant sort of way, that it was charming, but she was incapable of appreciating the effort. She felt faint. Parched. If Communion wine had been on offer, she would have taken an ecumenical step, confessed her sins and downed a swift gulp.

Service. Rose petals and rice. Photographs.

Josie said apologetically, 'There's a *vin d'honneur* next, to fob off hoi polloi who aren't going to make it onto the dinner list. The good news is, there'll be

something to drink.' They followed the wedding cavalcade, shimmering ahead of them in the haze of the afternoon heat.

The quiet country lanes were choked with cars
bumper to bumper, braking unpredictably, hooting as
they went. Once parked, their occupants scrambled out,
straggling over the rough stubble towards the woods,
where trestle tables had been set up in the deep shade of
a clearing, covered with paper cloths, and laid with cardboard plates of little cakes and biscuits and plastic
glasses. No bottles, Susan noted glumly.

'*Eh bien, madame.* How does this compare with an
English wedding?' The bridegroom's father proffered a
plate of biscuits. Susan cudgelled her brains for French
vocabulary.

'I think . . . we drink more,' she replied through a
mouthful of dry crumbs, before her social censor could
blank out the words. She looked embarrassed, but Yves
roared, nodding.

'I think you are right. We drink less in France than we
did. We all worry about our health. We drink less, and
there's the cholesterol, we worry about that, so we eat
less butter and cream – but don't let them hear you say
that in Normandy!'

Under the trees women sat primly on wooden benches

nibbling biscuits while the men stood about and smoked. More arrivals, more kissings and handshakes.

Josie, smiling affably, greeted a well-built local, tightly buttoned into his suit, turned back to Susan, the smile erased. 'That shit kept us waiting six months to repair the roof. Too busy. And the one who's heading this way now nearly gave me a nervous breakdown: we didn't have an inside water supply one entire holiday because of him, the swine. Had to wash under the hose –'

John had connected a length of hosepipe to an exterior tap and they had washed in turn under its bruising gush. Fun, in theory, but she recalled the ground growing slimy beneath her feet, the shock of cold water on chilly days, the sheer inconvenience of it all. As she attempted to rinse mud off her bare feet, or rubbed down the girls with towels dried to board-like stiffness in the sun, she had entertained brief, guilty dreams of package holidays, seaside flats with soft beds and en-suite bathrooms, hotels with running hot and cold room service.

She turned towards the plumber now, the man she had mentally hung, drawn and quartered, flayed, and thrown to the dogs that summer past. She managed a smile.

'We're so happy to have you back with us,' he exclaimed. 'You must tell us your news –'

Josie said hastily, 'You must meet my friend from London.'

'What a beautiful wedding!' Susan trotted out, the phrase now practised and fluent.

'Does she speak French?' he asked Josie.

A little way off, where the road curved round the edge of the woods, late arrivals filtered through the trees. A young woman was approaching, tripping gracefully across the uneven ground in platform soles with alarmingly high heels. Susan watched her with astonishment: dark bronze skin, suspiciously bright red hair, a dress cut so low that her firm, peachy breasts were almost completely exposed. Among the muted print frocks and village coiffures she looked as out of place as a bird of paradise in a cage of budgies.

In the deep, inviting cleft between her breasts a heavy silver crucifix nestled provocatively. The skirt was long and tight, walking made easier by the split from hem to crotch. Her bronze legs gleamed as she swayed towards them. She smiled, teeth flashing. Susan saw the bridegroom look over and flinch as though blinded for a moment by a bright light.

'Mme Marvel!' She arrived, breathless, laughing, and kissed the air a carefully spaced three inches away from Josie's cheek, ensuring that her own make-up and hair remained undisturbed.

'Lucienne!' Josie surveyed her with undisguised interest. 'You're very . . . elegant today.'

The girl smiled, pleased, and smoothed her hands over her hips, down the skin-tight skirt. She spoke in heavily accented English.

'Zer dress, my own design. Zer shoes. Versace. Poor Gianni . . .'

'Lucienne used to visit us with Stéphane,' Josie said, 'for English practice with the girls.'

'Ah! zat was a golden time!' The delivery was theatrical, overdone, yet Susan sensed the girl meant what she said.

' "Zey are not long, ze days of wine and roses –" '

'Lucienne! Poetry!'

'You made us learn some lines each week, remember?' She touched her breasts briefly, as though to reassure herself they were still there. 'I was so happy, then.'

Josie, standing close, saw shadows and the beginning of lines in the young face; a downward tug of dissatisfaction at the corners of the full mouth.

'And what are you doing, these days?'

'Oh, still I try to break into zer fashion world. But my husband want me to stop working so hard. He says, why bozzer if you do not have to?'

'You're married! I didn't know.'

'He is a –' she frowned, pursing her lips irritably,

'*marchand de ferraille.*'

'In the scrap business.' Josie patted the smooth brown arm. 'Well, he's obviously a success.'

Lucienne twitched her head in the direction of a burly man in jeans and check shirt standing alone on the edge of the crowd.

'Zer jeans are from Armani,' she pointed out help-fully, 'and zer shirt Ralph Lauren. So well cut. We came in zer Mercedes.' The golden eyes snapped with plea-sure, 'but we cannot stay. I just wanted to see Stéphane become zer good little husband.'

She glanced over at the bridal couple with their plas-tic glasses, toasting one another in fruit punch for yet another photograph.

'He was a *beau garçon*, a lovely boy.' She smiled, the teeth brilliant. 'Well, I must say hallo to some people. My mother is here somewhere but she and my old man –' she grimaced and drew a line across her throat. A sigh and a shrug. 'It's so boring, isn't it?'

'What?' Josie asked.

'Everything. Families. Life!' She burst into a peal of laughter that caused a few of the older ones to glance over and away, eyebrows raised. Then, with a wave she was off, swaying her way across the grass, pausing to bestow an air-kiss here, deliver a joke there – usually to one of the better-looking young men.

False Pretences

From the road beyond the trees there came the sound
of a powerful engine revving up; the unseen Mercedes
roared away, drowning the voices and laughter. Josie
saw that Stéphane's attention had slipped for a moment
as he glanced out into the brightness beyond the shade,
listening. When the roar of the engine faded into the
distance, the laughter seemed louder, as though re-
establishing its authority.

Zinc tubs of punch were circulating again when Susan
noticed a new group arriving, latecomers, waving to the
family, raising plastic glasses to the bride and groom.
Greetings were shouted across the clearing, good-
natured accusations – 'Late, as always!' – and a tall man
in a crumpled cream linen suit and grubby white sneakers made his way through the crowd, stopping for hugs,
kisses, jokes. As he progressed, the sound of laughter
spread out from where he stood, like ripples from a stone
dropped in a pool. She became aware, suddenly, that, on
the bench next to her, Josie had stiffened, was staring in
disbelief at the man in the pale suit. As though feeling
her gaze, he swivelled, raking the crowd, and caught
sight of her. He paused, head cocked in pleasure, and
came towards them through the trees, arms flung wide in
greeting and astonishment.

'My God,' Josie muttered. 'It's Nick.'

Then he was upon them, and whether she rose spontaneously to her feet or he pulled her up, however it happened, Josie was swept into an enveloping hug, an embrace that lasted a fraction longer than was necessary.

Then he held her away from him and said in a lazy drawl that she hadn't changed at all. Accusingly: 'You haven't got so much as a grey hair.'

'Oh I did have, when I was younger.'

He guffawed appreciatively, and then Susan saw the hesitation, the pause; the hiatus that can follow a hearty greeting when people have long been out of touch.

Josie, suddenly awkward with his hands still on her shoulders, half-turned, disengaging herself, gesturing.

'This is my friend Susan, from London. This is Nick. An old friend.'

He flinched extravagantly as though she had struck him. 'An "old friend"? Christ, Jo, is that what I've been demoted to?' He glanced about conspiratorially. 'Incidentally, am I safe? Where's old Thingy –'

'John died,' Josie said, timing it for when his smile was at its widest, a pantomime leer of lecherous complicity.

'Bugger,' he said, not at all put out. 'I was counting on a fisticuff situation before the night was out. Still, rotten for you. Condolences and all that stuff –'

'What are you doing here?'

'Family friend, love.'

She gave him a sceptical look. 'Since when?'

'About five years.'

Right after John died and she had stopped coming.

'I was staying with some Parisians a couple of miles outside the village –'

'Not the ones who've put steel patio doors in their barn –'

He pulled a rueful face. 'Sorry about that. The son's an ex-student of mine. They introduced me to Yves and it sort of went on from there . . .'

Susan sat swirling her drink, forgotten, part of the scenery. She was unresentful; this was just another example of the repertory theory of life. She had defined it once, to Josie: 'Each of us thinks we're the leading player in our drama, but at the same time, we're supporting characters, spear-carriers even, in another play, someone else's.'

In her personal sitcom she observed those around her with an ironic yet kindly eye; playing the part of the ill-dressed Englishwoman, aware of the small tragi-comedies being enacted around her; the figure in the background, the linchpin. Around her the wheel spun, she the still centre –

'So how do you know whether this one is your scene or theirs?' Josie had asked.

'You don't.'

Someone took a photograph, the shadowy woodland flashing into momentary brilliance. Who had been framed in the viewfinder this time? Was she in the shot somewhere, part of the crowd, helping to establish the scene, lending interest to the perspective?

The artist sets up his easel, gets to work. But what is he really painting?

In Assisi last year she had seen a fresco, possibly a Giotto, that captured a crucial rural moment: a peasant, poised high in a tree, is picking fruit, concentrating on the task in hand, reaching up, feet braced in the forked branches. The fruit is important, his role in its harvesting matters. Down in the piazza, in front of the church, a saint is taken to his burial with lamentations, but that's another story.

In Urbino, three men stand in the foreground of a certain small, much reproduced work by Piero della Francesca, robes glowing, hands, feet, faces disposed for the elegant group portrait they inhabit. What do they know or care about a flagellation going on in the rear left-hand corner? That's background. Someone else's suffering.

The field must still be ploughed, though Icarus falls from the sky.

Would today's show turn out to be a comedy or a

tragedy? And whose production were they all appearing in? Bit players in Stéphane's wedding, of course. But starring roles could be on offer for some in a parallel production.

The bench wobbled as Josie sat down again. Nick had wandered away back to his group. In his sneakers he stepped lightly, like a man walking on eggs, a tip-toe movement, weightless. Josie drained her plastic beaker.

'That was Nick.'

'So I gathered.'

Susan glanced up: Josie was looking towards the trees, watching the tall, pale-suited figure lead the way out to the sunshine like a Pied Piper.

At the side of the concrete block that was the village hall men were turning a whole sheep, slowly roasting in the open air. The charcoal glowed like opal, the grey dust veined with glittering fire. The skin of the sheep sizzled, crackling in the heat. Inside, the hall was transformed, the bald room grown bosky, its stark concrete walls hung with garlands of leaves. Four rows of trestle tables ran the length of the room, white cloths decorated with flowers and streamers. The benches from the *vin d'honneur* had found their way by truck and on roof-racks, to double as dinner seating.

'They used to put Chinese paper lanterns over the light bulbs on special occasions,' Josie said, distrait, 'then the council installed neon lighting.'

Susan restrained herself from saying it's all right, you don't have to talk to me, but they lapsed into silence anyway.

On the dais a local DJ was setting up a sound system, testing the microphone and checking the amps. Occasionally an electronic shriek or ear-splitting roar would shake the walls.

In the car Josie had fiercely scrubbed her face with a moist tissue. She had brushed her hair and hastily redone her face, all the while frowning horribly into the rear-view mirror, muttering repeatedly what a mess she looked, what a bloody *mess*.

Susan watched her now, admiring her cool, dark skirt and top, the way her dark hair clung, sculpted, to her head, the quick confidence of her movements. She had never realised Josie was a skilled actress: few, here, would have guessed she was in a turmoil.

The guests straggled about the room, establishing informal table-plans among themselves. Josie and Susan were drawn into a group at the far end of the room, not quite the top table, but well above the salt, seated among the family, with an uncle, a couple of cousins, a sister or two. Susan's headache grew worse. Trying to keep even a fingerhold on the eddies of conversation was proving a strain.

Like bees the guests gathered, clung, moved apart, re-formed, the buzz of talk louder now, the pace quickening. Eyes were bright with anticipation of the pleasures to come. Bottles of wine, red and white, stood between the baguettes and the mineral water. There was clapping, the first of many informal toasts, hot canapés, some cheers, faces a little flushed from heat. Shoes were cautiously eased from aching feet beneath the table-cloths, there was a sense of a collective loosening of corsets and braces. Local women began dumping vast platters of pâté and gherkins on the tables.

Susan gulped her wine. She scanned the room, slowly, picking up a head flung back in laughter, a grimace, a furtive nose-picking, a fumble beneath a blouse. Next to her, Josie was looking inward, lost in thought. The man seated next to Susan made a joke about the local wine, and she laughed obligingly. He introduced his wife, and they launched into an animated discussion of the British Royal family: was it true that the Queen was furious with . . .? Had Prince Philip really made that remark about . . .? From the corner of her eye Susan saw Nick rise from his seat, envelope a blue-suited neighbour in a flamboyant hug and head towards them, lazily elegant despite the creased suit.

He paused here and there to greet a local, shake a hand, pat a shoulder, then he was with them again. Somehow the table expanded to allow another chair, somehow it seemed fun, rather than irritating, that people should be squeezed up to make room for him, next to Josie, and at once Josie was requisitioned, lost to the rest of them.

Susan, head down, carefully cutting a gherkin into wafer-thin slices and then arranging the slices in a starburst pattern on her plate, shared their conversation perforce, without being part of it. After a while, in desperation, she leaned across the table and attempted to follow a discussion about government policy on vineyard upgrading.

Nick and Josie talked through the hors d'oeuvres and the asparagus. While everyone else seized hunks of spit-roast lamb from huge baking dishes, they went on talking. Through the salad and the cheese and towering *pièce montée* of profiteroles with caramel glaze they talked on, heads closer, voices lower. Nick refilled his glass, and Josie's, from time to time. When their bottle was empty, Susan passed them one from further down the table.

Later, Josie said, surfacing guiltily, 'We've been horribly rude.'

'Catching up,' he said.

'I haven't seen Nick for over twenty-five years. We were undergraduates together.'

Dangerously attractive, Susan acknowledged. He had an angular, witty face, high cheekbones and grey eyes of patent disingenuousness which he widened, cat-like, to make a point. She wondered how much he had changed over the years. His hair was grey but there was plenty of it, in a Roman emperor sort of cut, falling untidily onto his brow. He looked gleeful and wicked and intriguingly decadent.

'Students today, they're a feeble bunch. Remember Paris, in '68? The riots. Great days! We were there on the barricades, tearing up the cobblestones –'

'We did nothing of the kind!'

'I distinctly remember prising loose a cobblestone and hurling it at a particularly overweight *flic* –'

'You're such a fantasist, Nick.' Josie was laughing, her face soft and flushed with wine and pleasure.

'All in the past, darling. I'm a hardworking media tart these days.' He was including Susan now. 'I'm the tame Brit on French telly. When they want to know what perfidious Albion is *really* thinking, I'm their man. And when the old Beeb needs an opinion from the expat-on-the-spot, I zap over on Eurostar and give them my three-minute soundbite. So far they haven't sussed that I don't have a clue. But nobody else has a clue either, so –'

'What about that job lecturing in Sweden?'

'One winter was enough. It's bloody twilight there for half the year. I need the sun.' His hand rested on Josie's shoulder. 'Remember that year we worked for those grape-farmers in Provence, bringing in the *vendange?*

'I got bitten by the vine flies and Nick had to paint me with calamine to stop me scratching myself to death. I was white from top to toe, I looked like a zombie.'

'You looked like a Canova,' he said.

Susan's eyes flicked up to Josie's face. Would she catch a glimpse of embarrassment; discomfiture at this unequivocal baring of a private moment? But Josie's eyes were bright with long-ago sunlight.

'It was so hot, the smell of the grapes was like wine, we crawled through the vines, clipping and gathering; arms and legs aching, and our hands and mouths grew sticky with the juice, and the Spanish workers filled the baskets and the farmer kept shouting, keep going, keep going, there might be rain . . .'

'On the last day,' Nick said, 'there was a banquet. We lined up at the vats and tasted the *must*, and sat about stupefied. And then, as I recall, we –'

Josie put her hand over his mouth. 'I think that's enough.'

The DJ had got the sound system under control and

music was blasting out, deafening. The bride and groom took to the floor. The guests clapped and cheered. Josie shouted in Nick's ear, 'Susan and I went to Italy last year. In search of Veronese –'

'– chap who did the crumbling ruins –'

'No, not Piranesi –'

'Don't you love his *Stabat Mater* –'

'Nor Pergolese –'

'His best piece was *Six Characters in Search of* –'

'Not Pirandello –'

'– if you like medals and antlers –'

'Er . . . damn!'

There was a pause in the music. Josie turned to Susan: 'Sorry about this,' she said, sounding not the least bit sorry. 'It's a silly game we used to play. Circular references. Nick always won. As you can see.' She was laughing, her face pink.

Poor John, Susan thought. Now he really is dead.

'Can I take her away from you?' Nick was asking.

Susan stared at him, jolted. He waved at the dance floor. She smiled. 'Of course.'

'Give me five minutes.' Josie headed for the door marked, unambiguously, WC. There was a silence.

Susan gave him a quick, searching look. 'Have we met before?'

'We can't have, can we?'

'I suppose not. But . . . I thought you looked familiar for a moment.'

He yawned, not bothering to conceal it. 'You've known Jo quite a while, I imagine?'

Josie and Susan had met at one of those dinner parties where the hostess, faced with a single woman and unable to drum up a tame gay or widower to even up the numbers, settles for killing two unattached birds with one stone. Josie and Susan were seated together. They disagreed about art, education, food, movies, shoulder pads, politics and the possibility of free will. Then, offhand, Josie said, 'I'm being difficult. Sorry. My husband went and died on me and I haven't got anyone at home to argue with – the girls are being Understanding. Very boring of them.' Five years later they were still disagreeing about most things.

Susan realised Nick expected an answer. 'We met just after John died.'

'I meant to ask about that.'

'Cerebral haemorrhage. No warning. Then, bang.'

'That's John for you. Now, when I go, I'll be completely senile, probably incontinent and hang around for months till everyone's thoroughly sick of me. Once I've gone they can heave a sigh of relief and get on with living.'

Susan asked bluntly, 'What went wrong?'

'Us, you mean? I was late once too often. It's a way I have, of walking close to the edge. I missed a plane. A rather important plane. She'd had enough. Old John was there to offer the sterling virtues.' The lazy drawl, the grin, the quick flash of the pale grey eyes. 'She was the love of my life, of course.'

The dance floor was crowded. The DJ had moved on from rock to the music his audience clearly preferred: the old-fashioned beat of the *bal musette:* the waltzes, the slower rhythms of nostalgia.

Josie had been dancing for two hours, oblivious of the rest of the world, unaware of smiles, nods, nudges.

Susan studied Nick and wondered: is he good news or bad, this spring-heeled Jack, doing the *paso doble* in his crumpled linen suit? He had what Chekhov called a talent for life, that was clear enough, inspiring gaiety, making anything seem possible, but could he be another Music Man, materialising without warning and encouraging everyone to indulge their secret fantasies, their hopes, dreams, ambitions, setting the trumpets and the seventy-six trombones soaring – himself vanishing in a puff of smoke, while the rest woke up next morning with a hangover and a sense of betrayal? But the Music Man would say: if the dream had been lived, even briefly, he had shown that it could be done. Well, maybe. But fate had rendered Susan cautious, indeed over-cautious: to lose one parent could be regarded as unfortunate, to lose two, and while you still had some of your milk-teeth, well, it made you hesitant about turning corners too sharply. So she had never been a candidate for the three-card trick or the secret of the universe in return for a modest cheque in the post. She inhabited a niche labelled 'Retreat', but retreat had two meanings, one less comfortable than the other. 'I travel a lot,' she told someone once, but there had been journeys not taken and others which had delivered less than they promised.

In Moscow once, visiting Chekhov's tomb, she had picked up a leaf fallen from a tree planted nearby and put it in her pocket. Driving back to the hotel she held it out to the interpreter, hoping for a significant moment: 'Could this, by any chance, be from a cherry tree?' He took the leaf and glanced at it. 'Yes,' he said and threw it out of the window.

The music changed, the steps slowed. Nick loomed over his partner. Protective or predatory? Josie's head was tilted back, her eyes closed, arms wound round his neck. She was slender, graceful in the long, swallow-tail skirt and clinging top, her body arched against the linen suit.

The locals were surprised by the English couple, so unreserved, so unselfconscious, but there was affection too, and hope. Corks popped and foaming bottles of the local *vin mousseux* circulated. Yves handed one to Susan and they clinked glasses. Her headache had eased. Perhaps tonight they were celebrating more than the formalising of a youthful union. As the old song had it, this could be the start of something new. Another old song, a Charles Aznavour number, drifted through the room like a breeze, past the swaying couples on the dance floor, to the open door and the darkening sky.

Susan opened the shutters and golden light poured into the room, warming the cracked old terracotta floor tiles. She made coffee, toasted a slice of baguette and carried it all outside with a week-old *Sunday Times*. The silence settled round her.

What a curious direction the evening had taken. Josie, twirling her glass edgily, had begun with embarrassment, attempted reluctance, toyed with refusal, fallen into indecision and then – in Susan's view – madness. For Josie had certainly not been quite sane.

'What do you think I should do?' she had asked.

'I think you should go,' Susan lied, reciting her lines like a good supporting character.

So the stars zoomed off in Nick's sports car to see the sun rise over the sea at St-Jean-de-Luz a hundred miles away, and Susan drove Josie's car back to the house, as the wedding shifted gear again, with the departure of the bridal pair to their home of some four years, to be followed shortly afterwards by a score of guests demanding the traditional wedding night soup and wine.

Susan had slept well. The house creaked and moved as old houses do. A kitchen tap dripped slowly and musically into a metal dish with a regular ping! ping! ping! like the ringing of a tiny bell. There were mysterious rustlings, whether of birds in eaves or termites in rafters she was not sure, but she was unperturbed. This was a peaceful house.

And now, still alone, as the sun rode high overhead, pulling the shadows tight around the big lime trees, she felt remarkably at home.

Josie had told her how she and John had always 'walked the perimeter' at some point in their stay, checking the barbed-wire fence, seeing what new weeds had sprung up, what new molehills and mysterious burrows had appeared. Susan did it now, alone, discovering unsuspected treasure: fat black sloes on spiky bushes, cob-nuts ripening on trees at the edge of the wood, mint and fennel growing wild, scenting her footsteps; quinces, yellow and grey, looking diseased but capable of producing clear scarlet jelly if boiled with sugar and strained. Too early for blackberries, but the unripe fruit already weighed down the brambles. Around her the cicadas creaked and rustled their song.

She was in the kitchen, peering without great interest into the fridge, when she heard a car pull up outside and knock at the door.

A voice called, in French, 'Good morning! It's me, Yves.'

The bridegroom's father, a little bleary round the eyes but otherwise unimpaired, apologising for disturbing her.

Susan broke in: 'I regret, Josephine is not here —'

'I know.' (Of course. Country life. They knew everything.) 'I have come to invite you: the wedding continues. Joséphine should have told you —'

But of course she had. 'The worst horror,' Josie had groaned, 'is that the next day everyone gets together and eats the whole meal all over again. It's *Huis Clos*, you feel doomed to relive the affair over and over and over —'

Yves was saying cheerfully, 'We finish off the leftovers. It will amuse you.'

'Ah!' Susan began cautiously. 'When . . .?'

'Now!'

'But — my clothes —'

He indicated his faded shorts and T-shirt. 'But it's informal! I shall take you in my car to save you the drive.'

She thought: I feel exhausted. I won't know anyone. I'm not in the mood. I shouldn't leave the house without letting Josie know –

'I'll get my bag,' she said.

'You prefer to keep the shutters closed, I see,' he commented. 'That's good. The house will stay cool. I used to tell Joséphine, but she loves the sunlight, she leaves the shutters open.'

'I grew up in India,' Susan said. 'Nobody wanted the sun pouring in.'

Everything was different, this morning. Old clothes, sandals, no carefully made-up faces or slicked-down hair. No DJ, instead music of a different era streamed from the speakers, and already they were singing along with the old songs. Children ran about, batting at balloons and shrieking in their pointless way, and the women were busy in the community kitchen, putting the meal together again, this time to be eaten cold, with salad.

'Ah! The friend of Joséphine. Welcome!' Jeanne called in French, when Susan looked in.

'Can I help?'

'To be sure.'

The day spun by, punctuated by food and drink and noise. The adults played childish games while the children fell asleep in corners; Susan cleared dishes and carried plates in and out. Nobody was polite to her or wondered if she spoke French. Today she was part of the scene. She reached across and scooped a second helping of a strawberry gâteau she had missed the night before.

Josie had said something sobering yesterday, at the *vin d'honneur*, about village life. Life here, which she and John had always seen as rich and fulfilling.

'Actually,' Josie had burst out suddenly, 'I think it's parochial and boring. Look at the young ones, they're stifling here, they're longing to get away; and the old are shadowed with disappointment. They sit about, dreaming of escape routes not taken, adventures missed. The middle-aged ones live through and for their children and worry about their parents, sandwiched between two frustrated generations, hoping for the best and fearing the worst.'

'What a Pollyanna you are,' Susan had said drily, suspecting that Josie was right.

Now she thought differently. She looked at the faces around her, participating in a ritual as familiar as drawing breath. There were feuds, of course, secret trysts, scandals. And there were youthful rebellions: people shacked up together openly, had 'partners' with no nonsense about *fiançailles*. Their grandfathers had worn the blue cotton trousers and black berets of tradition; this generation wore unisex jeans and tattoos; here and there a boy sported an earring. But the rhythm of life was so steady that in the end they fell naturally into step.

People were dancing down at the far end of the room, espadrilles and shorts partnering cotton frocks.

'Susan!' called her neighbour of the dinner table, 'would you care to dance?'

Will you, won't you, will you, won't you, will you join the dance?

Would she?

There was a distant rumble of thunder, a gust of hot wind from the open door. For a moment, surrounded by the sound of many voices speaking a language not her own, Susan again felt a warp in time: she was five, surrounded by heat and noise, the smell of spice and flowers and the promise of rain.

She was loved.

'You must come again, now that you know us,' Jeanne said, 'stay longer. We are quiet here, of course, not like the city, but . . . there is always something to celebrate – the fourteenth of July, the fifteenth of August, the start of the hunting season, the *vendange* . . . it's a way of life.'

By the time they dropped her back the sun was looping to the west, reddening the gold of the fields. She made herself a cup of tea and thought about Josie, and about this house that Josie was selling. A leap of enormous daring had suggested itself to her. All her life Susan had shown prudence, chosen cautiously; impetuosity had never featured in her affairs. Now she contemplated an irrational act: buy the house. She could afford it; she was a woman of independent means, beneficiary of several modest wills – 'the upside of being orphaned,' she had said wryly, many years ago. She could lend the house to friends, spend long summers here, the shuttered rooms cool on hot days, the sturdy walls protecting her from storms. The climate was not gentle.

'When the rain starts drumming on the roof,' Josie had exclaimed, 'it's like a bloody monsoon.'

Which, for Susan, was one of its charms.

Up at the turn-off from the main road a car pulled into the grassy verge and stopped. Josie reached for her handbag.

'Thanks for lunch. And the cathedral. It was a lovely day.'

'How about tomorrow?'

'I can't leave Susan on her own again. Not fair.'

'Fuck Susan.'

'Charming. She came to keep me company.'

'A fiver I'm better at that than she is. Well?'

She had kicked off her sandals, last night, or rather, earlier this morning, when they got to St-Jean-de-Luz, and had run along the beach. She barefoot, Nick soaking his sneakers in the surf, both laughing uncontrollably. What were we laughing at? she wondered, now. What could have been so funny? And why were they there?

At the wedding, it had seemed the only thing to do.

'In all those years with old John,' Nick had challenged her, 'did you ever just, you know, say fuck it, and do something crazy?'

She never had, of course. Life with John did not consist of unconsidered leaps.

'That's why you're all knotted up,' Nick said. 'You need to let yourself go, do something unplanned. Go for it.'

'Such as?'

'Well . . .' The grey eyes sparkled. 'We could have a splash in the sea, make love and watch the sun rise. That would do to be going on with.'

'Ah, Niccolò,' she said, 'old Nick. Tempting me again?'

Her head filled with wine and music, giddy with happiness, she had begun to laugh. Of course, why not, let's go for it. And it had been just as he said. Nick, capering on the beach, his hair wild, a goblin figure in his pale suit. She had loved him so desperately, all those years ago; created fantasy encounters in which he reappeared, contrite, promising to be dependable, to be true. And perhaps it could be so at last. Perhaps this was that fairy-tale thing, the second chance, the wish come true, the happy ending.

He had pulled her down onto the sand, draping dried seaweed round her neck, a garland that rustled against her skin and smelled of the ocean. He had kissed her and pulled up her skirt and said, 'Christ, Jo, passionkiller knickers, the new secret weapon, eh?'

She had looked up at the stars, some blotted out by the dark shape of Nick's head as he bent to kiss her again.

After John's death, when she was getting to grips with widowhood, she had lunch one day with a woman whose husband had just gone off with a newer model. Alone and pushing fifty, the friend had confessed panic. 'What do you do about sex?' she asked, and Josie said, 'Not a lot,' and explained that the market was limited for women like them, unless they went in for the dubious casual encounter or afternoon tumbles with the available husbands of women they knew.

And the other woman said, 'I'll catch it on the wing then. Standards will have to be lowered, I suppose.'

Josie had forgotten that conversation until now, with Nick urgently attempting to divest her of her Marks & Sparks knickers. And she thought sadly: ah no! This was the man she had loved so fiercely that it hurt. And how much more painful it had been when she had decided she must stop loving him.

She squirmed out from under him and said, 'Nick, don't you think I'm a bit old for this?'

'No. Of course not.'

'Well then, aren't *you*? Is this what it's come down to? The party pick-up?'

He sat up, rubbing his back gingerly. He looked, she thought, slightly relieved.

'Never get divorced, love. It kills you.'

'As opposed to being widowed, which . . .'

He flinched, theatrically. 'Sorry, sorry.'

Josie was aware of a dull ache that seemed to fill her whole head; her eyes were sore and her mouth was dry. She stared at the grey horizon. 'Where's the bloody sunrise, then?' she asked fretfully.

'I'd allowed for a leisurely coupling and a post-coital fag. It'll be a while. I should have brought some wine.'

'You know what I'd really love? A hot drink. A coffee – no, *un chocolat*.'

He sprang up and pulled her to her feet. '*Un chocolat pour madame! Pas de problème.*' He stirred the sand disconsolately with a wet sneaker. 'Pity though. It'd have been nice to renew acquaintance with your private parts.'

Through the steamed-up window of the all-night bar Josie watched the sky growing pale, nacreous, the stars disappearing into the brightening blue of space.

'Do you see much of your boys?'

'No. Well . . . They drop in now and then. When they were younger, the Bitch, as I affectionately think of her, wouldn't let them near me. Officially I had access, but . . .'

'Do you want to talk about it?'

'No thanks.'

He ruffled his hair impatiently and she saw that the Roman cut was designed to combat a receding hairline.

'Oh, I've been wounded, darling. Don't let the laughs fool you. But I won't be showing you the scars.'

Refusing to play for sympathy at least. Was he deliberately doing a Coriolanus, or did she just read it that way?

'It's all your fault,' he said with grim humour. 'You banished me from Eden.'

'Come off it,' she said, but gently. 'You're the original snake in the grass.'

It was hot in the car. Josie felt perspiration break out on her scalp. She fiddled with her handbag to conceal a giveaway tremor, wanting to tell him she was scared. She looked at his hands on the wheel, the skin not as smooth as she remembered, but still beautiful. She touched his fingers, smiled unhappily.

He said, reading her, 'Can the leopard change his spots, that's what you're wondering. Well, who knows, love. But it could be fun, finding out.'

She got quickly out of the car and slammed the door.

'Jo! Don't run away.'

'Why don't you call me next time you're in London?'

He reached out and took her wrist, kissed her palm and folded the fingers over to hold the kiss in place; stroked her closed hand.

'Get yourself a better class of knicker.' The wicked eyes gleamed. He twitched his eyebrows, Groucho Marx fashion. 'That's a disinterested suggestion, by the way.'

About to be crisply feminist, she was trapped into laughter instead. He could always make her laugh.

She turned and walked away down the rutted lane towards the house, shaky on her high heels, stumbling on a loose stone, her steps unsteady. Behind her, the car drove away. No fairy-tale ending then. Just for a moment she saw Nick's grin, the grey eyes widening disingenuously, the light-stepping way he had of moving, hands held away from his sides, like a Greek about to break into a dance. Happy ever after would have been nice. She hoped she could stop crying before she reached the end of the lane.

Up at the turn-off from the main road Susan heard a car. It stopped, shielded by trees, and there was the faint slam of a door. A few moments later Josie came into view, walking down the winding lane. She was too far away for Susan to see her face but something about the set of her shoulders, the way she stumbled slightly at one point, sent a signal that the Music Man had indeed vanished in a cloud of exhaust fumes.

Susan had been taking some measurements: a porch outside the south-facing kitchen door would be perfect; keep off the fierce sun, and the rain in the stormy season. It could look charming, covered with creeper. She would call it a porch, but she would think of it as a veranda.

She began hastily to open the shutters to let in as much sunlight as possible. She wanted the place to look welcoming for Josie, though – good friend that she was – she would do her best not to look too buoyant herself. She would need to share the disappointment for a decent length of time before she allowed cheerfulness to break in.

Acknowledgements

'Trapped' was broadcast on BBC Radio 4.

'Hortus Inclusus' was published by *Punch*.

'A Sense of Isolation' was published by *London Magazine*.

Versions of the following stories were published: 'The Sugar Palace' in *Chowkidar 1977–1997*; 'A Small Request' in *Church Times*; 'Tango' in *You* magazine; 'A Visit to the Zen Gardens' in *Woman & Home*.

'Reading Lessons' was a prizewinner in the Commonwealth Foundation short story competition for radio.